MW00416574

Matching Wits: Amish Matchmaker: Book Five

Copyright © Samantha Bayarr 2019

Scripture quotations are from the New King James Version of the Bible.

A NOTE FROM THE AUTHOR

While this story is set against the backdrop of an Amish community, the characters and the town are fictional. There is no intentional resemblance between the characters and community in this story and any real members of the Amish or communities. As with any work of fiction, I've taken license in some areas of research as a means of creating the necessary circumstances for my characters and the community in which they live. My research and experience with the Amish are quite knowledgeable; however, it would be impossible to be entirely accurate in detail and description since every community differs, and I have not lived near enough the Amish community for several years to know pertinent and current details. Therefore, any inaccuracies in the Amish lifestyle and their community portrayed in this book are due to fictional license as the author.

Thank you for being such a loyal reader.

TABLE OF CONTENTS

CHAPTER ONE

Lettie Fisher stood in front of her class, trying to get them to settle down after the excitement of seeing four wild turkeys running around their playground. "Eli King; time to take your seat!" she said to her most challenging student.

The school year had barely begun, and already, he was trying her patience.

Truthfully, Eli reminded her very much of his *Onkel* Luke, who spent his days disrupting class when she was trying to learn in this very school. Every day Luke would get into trouble on some level, and sadly, he often tried to involve Lettie with his antics. Though she sympathized with Luke, she turned her back on him, thinking that ignoring his bad behavior would make him stop, but she'd learned too soon that those methods did not work with the stubborn boy.

Now that she was the teacher, she found those same methods did nothing to deter young Eli, who acted as if he wanted to follow in his uncle's reputation. Luke had been taking care of Eli since his older brother had fallen ill and could no longer handle the upkeep of his farm or his *kinner*. Now that the man had passed away, Luke had inherited the responsibility for the twins. Eli's twin sister, Ellie, was quiet and one of Lettie's star students. If not for the same dark blonde hair and freckles the children shared, one would not know they were related in the least.

"I have to go out and round 'em up so I can take 'em home; *mei dat* would be so proud of me," Eli insisted. "By Thanksgiving, they'll be big 'nough to eat!"

They're plenty big enough to eat now, she thought.

5

Eli's father had passed away just before school started, but the child continued to talk about him as if he were still with him and his twin sister, Ellie. How would Thanksgiving be for the children without their father? She worried about the child, who only wanted his father to be proud of him, but was Eli aware that his father could no longer have an opinion of him or his behavior?

Regardless of his apparent need to mourn, Lettie couldn't have him disrupting the class with his quest to earn approval from a deceased parent. She believed Luke had sent the children to school too soon after their father's passing, but that was not her business. She knew that the Bishop had stood behind his decision, thinking it was best if the children didn't get behind in their studies, but Eli was falling behind even though he'd been here every day since school reconvened the first week of September.

"I think your eyes are much bigger than your stomach, Eli," Lettie said to the boy. "If they're meant to be eaten at your supper table come Thanksgiving, which nearly two whole months away, you'll be able to catch them between now and Thanksgiving. But wait until after school. Until then, you need to get back to your seat and prepare for the spelling test I'll be giving in about ten minutes."

Eli's eyes were anxious with a desire for those wild turkeys. "But if I don't get 'em penned up now, they'll be gone back into the woods by the time school lets out," he complained. "I promise I'll be right back after I run 'em home."

Lettie gave the boy a firm shake of her head and aimed her gaze at his desk in the second row. He was her most wiggly second-grade student and way too old to be arguing and giving her a headache so early in the school day. She'd concluded part of his constant distraction was due to the problems at home; the poor child had not had a mother since she'd died giving birth to him, and now he'd recently lost his father. She wondered if he wasn't ready to start school, but when she'd addressed her worries to the Bishop, he'd insisted Eli and Ellie should get back to normal as quickly as possible and starting out the school year by being behind the rest of the class was not the answer.

His sister, Ellie, had taken the opposite approach to the trouble at home and had become quiet and withdrawn. She was a bright student and had never given Lettie a moment of concern; she was, in fact, the opposite, being overly helpful all the time, and that worried her too. Lettie didn't know how to help either of them except to keep teaching them. She'd wanted to take food to the family, but her history with their Uncle Luke kept her from reaching out to them. The Bishop's wife had asked her twice already to take a turn bringing them a meal, but each time she'd managed to create an excuse strong enough that she almost believed it herself. Truthfully, she still held onto a grudge against Luke, though her heart betrayed her where that man was concerned.

Lettie made the mistake of turning her back Eli to help another student, but the roar of laughter that filled her classroom let her know he was up to something.

"Look at him go!" one of the students said, pointing out the window.

Lettie gazed out into the schoolyard to see what all the commotion was, disappointment clouding her mood when she spotted Eli out there chasing the wild turkeys. How had he managed to escape the classroom without her noticing? Though she had to admit he was entertaining, her priority was to keep her classroom a place of learning for the sake of the rest of the students. She bit her bottom lip to keep from laughing at the child who was not much bigger than the turkeys he was chasing. They flapped their wings, trying to carry off their rotund frames; she had to admit they were looking mighty tempting to her right now even though it was only the first week of October. She loved Thanksgiving, but she had no idea if her parents planned to stay for the holiday in Grabill with her sister, Annie, and her husband and four children. They'd been there since summer, leaving Lettie alone in the family home. All her close friends were too busy with their families to consider inviting her for the holidays—except maybe Cassie, but even she'd recently gotten married and had two small babies to care for. The last thing she would want to have hanging around during the holidays was the community schoolteacher and resident spinster, even though she and Cassie were the best of friends.

Lettie felt a gentle tug on her sleeve; it broke her gaze from the entertainment Eli provided his classmates. At her side, Ellie's tearful blue eyes nearly broke her heart.

"Please let Eli get the turkeys home; he ain't big 'nough to hunt this year, and *Dat* never got a chance to teach him before he..." she let her voice trail off, but Lettie understood what she was trying not to say.

Lettie swallowed the lump clogging her throat; how could she say no to an argument like that? She nodded and smiled at Ellie, but she wasn't expecting the child to throw herself into her arms with such a robust hug.

"*Danki,* Miss Lettie," Ellie sniffled.

Lettie hugged her back, feeling it was the least she could do for the family; if getting those turkeys would help Eli to believe his father would be proud of him and help him deal with his grief, how could she object with a clear conscience?

She glanced out the window at the eager boy, who swooped his arms toward the turkeys, herding them in the direction toward his farm just down the road from the school. If he were half as determined to learn his math as he was about getting those large birds back home, Eli would be as bright a student as Ellie. But settling down to studies didn't seem to be the way of the *menner* in the King family. Luke and his older brother, Jeremiah, had both quit school the day their own father passed away. She prayed it would not be the same for Eli since Luke didn't make it past the sixth grade, though Jeremiah had almost finished eighth grade. The boys quit school to care for their mother, who shut down after the death of her husband. Most in the community said she'd suffered from a broken heart; she'd died just after Jeremiah's eighteenth birthday, leaving him to care for Luke alone. They'd led a hard life, and she didn't wish that on the twins.

Lettie had no idea what it was like to lose a parent, so it was tough for her to relate to the children's grief. Unsure of whether it was hurting or helping to let the boy chase the wild turkeys, she wondered if there was something more she could do for them. Perhaps it was time for her to put her dislike for Luke away with her childhood and take the family a meal. All the other women in the community had taken a meal to them, and she was running out of excuses to put off her turn at doing the neighborly thing for them. She had acted selfishly. After all, it was more for the children than it was for Luke, even though it would benefit him too. They lived on the family farm that Luke's father had built, and Luke had never left home because he and his brother took over their father's business after he'd passed away. Luke had lived in the *dawdi haus* while his brother was still alive, but she had to assume he'd moved into the main house since then.

It was only one visit and one meal; why was she so nervous about it? Was she worried that Luke would invite her to join them, or was she more worried that he might not?

****

Lettie glanced at the clock on the wall above her desk; Eli had been gone almost an hour. She wrung her hands with worry; what could be taking him so long? It was nearly the noon-hour; should she dismiss the class instead of having them break for lunch and recess? If she dismissed them early, she could check on Eli, but she would have some explaining to do with the Bishop over an early dismissal. She could give Ellie a ride home as an excuse to go by their house to see if everything was alright. What had she been thinking of letting Eli run off chasing four wild turkeys? Every minute that ticked by filled her with fear that something might have happened to him. Would she find him by the side of the road hurt and attacked by the giant birds? Panic seized her as her mind reeled with one bad scenario after another involving the large birds.

As she opened her mouth to announce an early dismissal, an approaching buggy interrupted her. Squinting against the midday sun, seeing Luke in his open buggy caused her heart to flutter. Eli was seated beside him. She put a hand to her chest and tried to breathe. Though she was relieved to see Eli was alright, she hadn't prepared herself for a meeting with Luke.

That man gave her heart palpitations every time she was near him, and she made a fool of herself, stumbling over her words every time she tried to talk to him. When she did manage to speak, the words usually came out in a snarky tone; she was certain that it turned his head away from her. He was too handsome to be single, and she didn't want him thinking she was going to throw herself at him like a desperate spinster—even if she was one.

Looking at her apron, which was crisp white when she'd arrived at school this morning, she felt irritation rise from her gut that she could do nothing to clean the yellow chalk dust that now covered it. She slapped at the front of it, trying to clean it before Luke saw her looking so messy, but she only managed to make it worse. It had been a chaotic morning, and her unkempt appearance would surely give away how frazzled his nephew's antics had made her. Would she be able to convey that to Luke, or would he bring out the worst in her as he tended to do? Not only did she get tongue-tied every time he was around, but he always found her in a frazzled and messy state—her dirty apron and flyaway hair proof of that.

She pushed her auburn hair behind her ear and threw her hands up and pasted on her best smile when Luke hopped down from the buggy and headed toward the door of the school with Eli. She was not going to be able to escape having him see her like this, so she determined not to let it bother her. Was she capable of remaining calm in his presence? She was about to find out.

Lettie pulled in a deep breath and let it out with a whoosh, hoping it would help her to let go of the tension that knotted up her stomach, but it didn't work. So, she checked her smile and walked toward the back of the classroom, hoping if she could head him off at the door, he wouldn't come in, or if he did, he wouldn't stay long.

Luke managed to get inside the door before she could get there without running like a mad-woman and scaring the children. The corners of her mouth dipped into a frown when her gaze met with his, but she quickly lifted them back into a forced smile. Neither of them said a word—they just stared.

Eli broke the spell between them. "I'm sorry I took so long getting back to school, Miss Fisher," he said with downcast eyes, but his remorse quickly shifted to a mischievous smile. "I lost two of 'em along the way, but I got two of them wild turkeys home, and *Onkel* Luke was so surprised!"

That brought a genuine smile to Lettie's face. "I'm so glad you made your *onkel* happy with the turkeys. Why don't you grab your lunch pail; we were just about to go outside to eat our lunch."

Eli scrambled to get his lunch pail from the pegs along the back wall of the schoolroom. Lettie ignored Luke and turned to the rest of the class, and clapped her hands together. "It's lunchtime; we'll be taking lunch outside on the picnic tables since this will be one of the last few nice days of the year so we can eat outside."

The class cheered as they ran toward the pegs; they grabbed their things and whisked by her and Luke, who was still standing there as if he wanted to talk to her.

She turned to him and pasted her smile back on. "Was there something else you needed, Mr. King?"

He leaned in and whispered. "Don't you think you should discipline Eli for running out in the middle of the day?"

Lettie pursed her lips, embarrassment, causing heat to rise to her cheeks. "I didn't see any harm in letting him chase the turkeys home; he told me his *Vadder* would be proud of him for getting them; it meant so much to him, and I believe children should follow their hearts as long as it doesn't cause them or anyone else harm."

"But he's been using that excuse ever since Jeremiah passed away. Lately, every time he gets into trouble, he says his *dat* wouldn't get mad at him; it's become a crutch. Didn't he disrupt your class by running out?"

Lettie bit her bottom lip to keep from smiling; she had to admit it was a clever excuse. "It wasn't the usual morning, I admit, but he's back, and hopefully, there won't be any more distractions."

"I need him to stay at school, and I need you to make him behave. I seem to remember getting into a lot of trouble when I was his age and older because I couldn't control my impulsive behavior. If you don't take care of it now, he's only going to get worse."

Was he trying to tell her how to run her class, or did he find her inadequate as the teacher of his nephew?

"Did getting into trouble make you stop, or did it make you eager to push the limits farther?" she asked.

Luke pursed his lips, but not to hide a smile.

She must have sounded as if she were reprimanding him for his past; it was in the past, but she didn't have any reason to believe he wasn't just as impulsive as an adult as he was when they were children.

"My point is that I just spent the past fifteen minutes lecturing him about not leaving

18

school, and you just let him off the hook," Luke said.

She gave a quick nod and raised her chin. "I planned to make him stay after school to make up for the test he missed while he was busy running off, but I figured I would send a note home explaining my disciplinary measures."

Luke raked his fingers through his thick blonde hair and sighed. "It's not been easy taking over the twins' care since *mei brudder* passed away, but I'm their guardian, so any problems or other needs will have to be brought directly to me from now on. I don't trust Eli to bring home any notes, and I don't think you should either."

Lettie swallowed down the lump in her throat; she shouldn't have been so short with him. He must be having a difficult time facing the loss of his brother and taking on the responsibility of the man's children without having the teacher giving him a lecture.

"I'm sorry for the added stress you're under at this time," she said, lowering her tone.

"I'll be keeping Eli after school today if that won't interfere with his chores at home."

"*Danki,*" Luke said, barely lifting his gaze from the floor. "You do what you have to, but I need you to promise me you won't let him get away with a stunt like this again."

Lettie nodded and pasted on a smile; she was helpless to abide by the man's wishes. Short of strapping Eli to his chair and putting horse blinders on him, she had no idea how she was going to keep the curious child from becoming distracted and disrupting the class again.

CHAPTER TWO

Lucas King sat on the front porch of the matchmaker, nervous as an unbroke horse. "I'm the only one who can raise Jeremiah's *kinner*," he explained. "I'm their only relative, and besides, I promised Jeremiah. *Mei brudder* asked me to take on the responsibly for the twins, but I can't raise them alone. It's only been a month since his passing, but I can't do it alone anymore. They need a *mudder*—especially Ellie. I don't know anything about raising girls, and that poor child tries to do all the cooking and cleaning after school and on weekends. *Mei brudder* wanted his *dochder* to have a childhood, not to be the woman of the *haus* at such a young age."

"I can see your need for a match," Miss Sadie said, sipping her meadow tea. "Do you want a match in name only?"

"I don't know how much time I'll have for courtin' since I'm doing so much work at home," he said. "If I get a bride in name only, I can move back out to the *dawdi haus,* and she could live in the main *haus* with the *kinner.*"

Luke hadn't thought that far ahead; he'd only had eyes for one woman ever since he'd become aware of the fairer sex, but Lettie Fisher despised him no matter how much he'd tried to get her attention when they were in school. Now that she'd been the teacher for the past few years, he'd assumed she had no interest in getting married. Besides, he saw Lettie as being too smart for her own good, and it intimidated him. Seeing her at the school only a few minutes ago when he marched Eli back to class had rendered him speechless; he'd made a fool of himself trying to talk to the lovely schoolteacher. He loved her, and expecting her to marry him in name only would not just insult her; it would hurt her, and she couldn't do that to her.

When he'd been at the school to discuss Eli, she'd looked at him with disdain, as though Eli's antics reflected his own reputation for being the class disruptor in his day. It was true; he'd gotten himself into more trouble than his father could handle, but he didn't lack for learning; he simply didn't enjoy being confined to a desk and chair all day. Like Eli, he preferred to be outdoors, enjoying nature and whatnot. Lettie Fisher always had her nose stuck in a book, and he didn't like to read—mostly because he didn't have the time or patience for it. Aside from Bible reading, Luke couldn't remember the last time he'd picked up a book. Reading never helped him with farming or tending to the stock, so he didn't see any point in it. He'd learned all he needed about farming from his father and grandfather. They'd learned from past generations, and none of them had had much book-learning, and they'd turned out just fine. Lettie's intelligence intimidated him and was another reason they probably wouldn't make a smart match.

Now, as he sat on the porch of the matchmaker, she was suggesting the one woman he wanted more than anything but didn't believe he could ever have.

Luke shook his head. "You'll be wasting your time trying for Lettie Fisher. She wouldn't marry me if I was the last *mann* on earth."

"What would make you say that?" Miss Sadie asked.

"For starters, I just left the schoolhouse to drop Eli back after he ran away from the schoolyard to chase a couple of wild turkeys home," he began. "And I practically yelled at her and told her how to run her class. I made her promise not to let him get out of control anymore, but the truth is, I don't know how to get him to stop acting out the same as I did when I was in school. It's only gotten worse since his *dat* died. But Lettie and I have a history from our school days that goes beyond what happened just a few minutes ago; her animosity toward me goes way back!"

His voice trailed off and the matchmaker gave him a minute to compose himself before continuing the conversation.

"I'm sure he'll settle down once you get a woman in the *haus* to care for their everyday needs. I will give the matter of your match some thought," she said. "But in the meantime, I would like to request your help with something, if I may."

Luke's eyes gaped with curiosity. "You want *my* help?"

"I wonder if I might ask you to repair the broken window at the schoolhouse," she said. "Since I am on the school board, it is my responsibility to get someone to repair it."

Luke nodded after a moment. "I'm handy enough that I can fix a window. I can go over there in the morning and see what needs to be done," he said. "I'll go over early when the *kinner* go to school."

Too bad I can't go before the teacher gets there! Wait a minute; is this a trick to get me to spend time with Lettie? He smirked. *It won't work!*

Miss Sadie smiled. *"Danki,* your services will be most helpful. It is getting colder every day, and the window needs repairing before the first snow."

Luke bid the matchmaker goodbye and went on his way after she promised to find him a suitable match. He didn't believe she'd have much luck with finding him one, but he had to hold onto the tiny bit of hope for the sake of the children. Though he had his heart set on Lettie, he would take whatever he could get and sacrifice his own happiness for theirs.

****

Lettie finished grading Eli's paper, discouragement crowding her thoughts. She'd had to reprimand him several times for daydreaming out the window, and it hadn't improved his test score any. He didn't lack in smarts at all; what he lacked was the skill to concentrate. Would that come for him with maturity, or would he be a daydreamer through school the way she remembered Luke being? Was there a way to fix this situation with Eli without involving Luke? Perhaps when she took the boy home, she would have to put her nervousness aside and speak to the man for the sake of her student and ask for his help in planning to get his nephew into a better frame of mind for learning. She didn't relish the idea of getting her stomach all churned up with butterflies, but he was a kind man now that he'd grown up some. Maybe it was time for her to put his childhood antics out of her mind and leave them in the past, though that would involve forgiving him for all the tricks he'd played on her when they were in school. Cassie had always told Lettie that Luke picked on her because he liked her, but in her opinion, that was a terrible way to show a person you liked them. He was handsome and made her stomach twist up in knots every time she was around him, but she still judged him on his school-boy behavior, and perhaps it was time she stopped doing that.

"I'm afraid you barely passed the test, Eli," she said.

Eli shrugged and walked toward the back of the class to get his coat and lunch pail. Did he not care that his nephew was barely passing? What did he care about, if not his family? Making his father proud of him? Was there a way to use that father-son pride to get him to improve his concentration and learning? Perhaps she should talk to Luke about that before using such a strong tactic against the child. She wasn't his parent or guardian, and she didn't want to risk having such a firm measure backfire on her. It would upset her if something she did made things worse for the child.

****

Lettie drove the short distance to the King farm, hoping she wouldn't have to hunt Luke down once she got there. She would have to ask Eli to fetch him if she didn't readily see him. She stopped her horse and looked around while Eli hopped down and tried to scurry off.

"Will you please go and get your *Onkel* Luke for me," she called after Eli. "I need to talk to him."

Eli waved behind him, and she hoped that meant he was going to get him. Luke exited the barn as the child approached and put up a hand to her. She lifted hers halfway and gave a shy wave. As he walked toward her, she started to step down from the buggy when she felt a strong hand on her arm to assist her. Luke's hand reached for hers, and she relinquished control to allow his assistance. She wasn't used to having anyone help her into or out of her buggy, but his warm hand made her hand tingle all the way to her elbow.

Focus, Lettie; remember why you're here.

"*Danki* for bringing Eli home," Luke said. "How did the test go?"

Lettie turned toward Eli, who was just inside the barn picking up the milk pail and took it inside, and she had to assume he was going to milk the cow as his afternoon chore. Once he was out of earshot, she turned her attention back to Luke though she found it difficult to concentrate with his smiling blue eyes staring right through her. His royal blue button-up shirt clung to his muscular arms and chest, and she had to look away when she detected the contours of his abs.

She cleared her throat. "I'm afraid he didn't do well on the test at all," she admitted. "I was generous with one of the harder questions and gave him extra points, but even with that, he barely passed."

Luke chuckled. "But, at least he passed it!"

Lettie pursed her lips and blew out a breath; was the man capable of taking education seriously?

"Only by a small margin," Lettie tried to warn him. "If he's to pass the second grade, he'll have to do better than barely passing grades. He spent most of the time during the test gazing out the window; that's why we're back so late in the day."

Luke pulled a pocket watch from his broadfall pants and checked the time. "I hadn't realized it was so late."

"I'd like to ask your opinion about something," Lettie said, using caution with her words. "About Eli, of course."

Judging by the expression on Luke's face, she'd have to say she'd just fed his ego a generous helping of humble pie with her own ego as the filling.

"Nothing seems to motivate Eli except his drive to please his *vadder,*" she began. "Perhaps if we encouraged him to make his *vadder* proud by doing better in school, that might make a difference."

Luke didn't say anything; he just stared off toward the pasture, and Lettie began to shift between her feet and stared at the ground. She chided herself for saying the wrong thing; she could see in his eyes she'd hit a nerve by talking about his dead brother. When was she going to learn to converse with people instead of being so socially awkward? She was aware that her social skills were lacking because she preferred to read and remain in fictional worlds where it was safer, but she'd really gone and stuck her foot in her big mouth this time.

"I'm sorry, Luke," she said, barely above a whisper. "I shouldn't have suggested such a thing."

"You're on to something there," he said. "But I don't think that's quite the right approach; back when I was in school, if the teacher would have told me that stopping my daydreaming and concentrating on my studies

31

would have made *mei vadder* proud of me, it would have made me think the opposite. As in, if I couldn't stop and do better in school, then *mei dat* would be disappointed in me. We don't want Eli thinking his *dat* is disappointed in him, or he might get worse and think there's no hope. I don't want to discourage him; we need to come up with a way to turn school into a positive experience, or he'll always make bad grades."

Lettie swallowed the lump in her throat. "I didn't think of that angle; you're right. The last thing I want is for Eli to feel bad about himself or like a failure if he can't make his *dat* proud of him. I guess that's one of the reasons I let him run after those turkeys today. I really felt bad for him."

"I agree with you that we need to find something that motivates him," Luke said. "But that is not the right way. I'm glad you came to me with this before saying anything to Eli."

Lettie blew out a breath; at least Luke wasn't angry with her for suggesting it. He'd even thanked her for coming to him first.

"Do you have any suggestions that might help?" she asked.

She wanted to ask what might have helped him back when he was having trouble, but she didn't want to insult him by bringing up his troubled past.

"I'll have to give it some thought," he said. "Perhaps if we both come up with a couple of ideas and then brainstorm a little about it, we can come up with something that might make a difference. Who knows; maybe if we work together, we can come up with a solution."

Lettie's cheeks heated at the prospect of working alongside Luke to help Eli. She'd never been competitive, but she suddenly found herself wanting to come up with the best solution for Eli. As his teacher, she believed it was her responsibility, but as a woman, she didn't like the idea of having to partner up with Luke.

CHAPTER THREE

Luke bundled up the children and helped Ellie into the buggy and drove them to school. He'd tossed around most of the night thinking about Lettie, and now he yawned repeatedly in the fresh morning air. He'd already put in almost a full day of work on the farm, hoping if he'd get the chores done early, he'd have enough time to talk to Lettie about Eli after he finished with the window.

When he got there, Lettie hadn't arrived yet, so he let himself in and put some wood in the stove to heat the classroom. It was a chilly morning, and Luke suspected they might have had their first frost last night. The sun had been up for two hours and was just warm enough to melt the frost from the grass in some spots, but there was still a hint of it under the shade of the large oak tree in the schoolyard.

"Why don't you clean the blackboard for Miss Fisher," Luke suggested. "It looks like she didn't have time before she went home yesterday."

Eli let out a groan, but Luke pointed a finger toward the blackboard. "Miss Fisher will be pleased with you for helping her out."

That brightened his face, causing him to pick up the large eraser and begin the task of wiping down the board. He pulled her desk chair up to get the spots he couldn't reach even on his tiptoes.

Ellie took the broom from the corner of the room and began to sweep the floor without being told. There was something to say about those two; they were as opposite as a tame pony and a stubborn mule. Luke hadn't missed the smile that crossed his nephew's face when he mentioned how happy the teacher would be with him if he helped her. Perhaps there was something to Lettie's idea of using his need to please others to get him to do what he was told. The only problem with that was Luke believed there was a fine line between being a people-pleaser and doing someone a kindness, and he did not want his nephew to turn into a self-imposed doormat to anyone. The boy had a good heart, but it had been broken recently, and that made him vulnerable; he would have to be careful about how he handled the boy's recent trouble at school. Though the child needed structure and discipline, he also required understanding and patience, but above all, he needed love. He certainly had plenty of that for the twins, but he had a hunch they'd be much more complete with a woman around to be their mother. All children needed a mother, didn't they?

****

When Lettie arrived at the school, she hadn't expected to see Luke's buggy there. Had he thought of something to help Eli? Whatever it was, his unexpected visit had her feathers in a ruffle too early in the morning. She parked her buggy under the tree, knowing that her horse would want shade before school let out for the noon hour.

When she entered the classroom, she noticed Eli standing on a chair, erasing the day's lesson from the board. Her breath hitched, and her hand flew to her mouth. Eli turned abruptly, panic in his eyes when he saw her.

"Did I do something wrong, Miss Fisher?" he asked.

"Nee," she said, trying to keep her composure. "I'm surprised to see you being such a big help to me; I'm proud of you!"

Eli smiled and then looked at his uncle Luke, who was stoking the fire in the woodburning stove. He looked up, and his blue eyes bore a hole right through her.

Oh, what that man did to her insides.

She turned her focus back to Eli; she couldn't tell the child he was nearly finished erasing the lesson that took her over an hour to put up on the board yesterday afternoon after school. He'd been so busy daydreaming when he should have been finishing his math test yesterday that he probably hadn't noticed her writing it all out during his testing time. The boy was so proud of himself for helping her that she didn't have the heart to let him see the disappointment hiding behind her smile. Luke flashed her a funny look, but she pasted on a smile so he wouldn't know the truth either. She would have to take the time to rewrite it during recess, and she would have to come up with a new lesson plan to take its place for the morning.

"I'm sweeping the floors, Miss Fisher!" Ellie said with a smile.

"I see that," she answered the girl with a big smile. "I'm so lucky to have *three* big helpers this morning. How did I get to be so lucky?"

She walked closer to the stove and held her hands out toward the warmth of the fire.

"The matchmaker asked me to fix the broken window," Luke answered as he put another couple of logs on the fire.

"The matchmaker?" Lettie asked. No sooner had the question left her lips than she regretted giving in to her curiosity. She didn't want him to see the worry in her face about his encounter with the matchmaker, but she hoped he didn't go to see her purposely—to find a match.

"I went to see her to get a match," he said without looking up.

There it was; her heart was sinking to the floor, and her lungs deflated.

"I need a *fraa,* and the *kinner* need a *mudder.*"

Ach; is that why he's really here?

The matchmaker had her methods of matching couples, and they usually involved a little bit of evasive action.

I wouldn't put it past the older woman to send him over here, thinking it would bring me and Luke together. Surely, the woman has taken pity on me for being too old to marry, but is Luke my only hope? Ach, Lord, I know it isn't a kind thing to wish for, but I don't want him to find a match—at least I don't think so.

It was evident to Lettie that Luke hadn't asked for her to be considered as his bride, or he would have asked her for a buggy ride before now. He certainly would have asked her before paying the matchmaker a visit.

"Jah, I keep forgetting she's on the school board," Lettie said, trying not to let her worry show. "*Danki* for agreeing to fix the window; it will soon be too cold in here to put up with a broken window. And *danki* for putting a fire in the stove; the *kinner* will be happy to come in out of the cold after walking here."

He nodded and then went out to get his tools from his buggy. Lettie opened her lesson book and searched for something else to begin her day, so she didn't look like an unprepared fool in front of Luke. She had no idea how long he would be here fixing the window, but she suddenly wished he would leave. Her emotions were torn between throwing herself at him and offering to be his wife and throwing him out of her classroom for not asking her first.

With her nose stuck in her lesson plan, she didn't see when Luke returned with an armful of firewood until the load tumbled to the floor in a heap. Lettie bolted from her chair with a start, her hand flying to her chest as if she was suffering a mild heart attack. She kept it there, trying to catch her breath.

"Sorry, I didn't mean to drop the wood and make such a racket," he said, ruffling Ellie's hair. "I was trying to avoid tripping over this little one when she bent down to sweep under the desks."

Lettie drew in a deep breath. *That's okay; I think you might have just taken five years off my life!*

Luke scooped her up and flew her around in a circle, making her laugh. It brought a smile to Lettie's face to see how good he was with the children. Though she enjoyed having them in her class, she couldn't imagine herself as their mother—not that she should imagine such a thing, but it was tough not to. Especially after Luke's shameless announcement about the matchmaker finding him a wife. Did he say that as a matter of fact, or had he said it get her

41

thinking? Perhaps Cassie had been wrong, and Luke never liked her at all. She'd never admit to liking him either, but his announcement stung more than she could have imagined.

****

When school let out, Lettie went straight to Cassie's house instead of going home. She had news to share with her best friend, and she didn't know how much longer she could keep it in without screaming.

"I need to talk to you!" Lettie blurted out as soon as Cassie opened the door, a child in each arm.

Lettie reached for Simon, and he gurgled at her as she took him from her friend.

"As you can see, I have my hands full, as usual, but I've always got time for you—as long as you don't mind giving me a hand—I seem to be lacking a much-needed extra pair of hands lately," Cassie said. "I was hoping you'd come by this week because I have so much to tell you."

Lettie didn't miss the shy smile on Cassie's face or the pink in her cheeks. "I can see married life if finally putting a smile on your face!"

"Jah," Cassie said. "Ben and I are finally a true couple!"

Lettie sucked in her breath, her eyes wide. "You mean you...?"

Cassie smiled and giggled and lowered her face to hide the pink in her cheeks. "You need to get married, Lettie; it is the best thing to happen to a woman!"

Lettie sighed and twisted at her apron strings; she had to tell someone her problems, and if anyone would understand her dilemma, Cassie was the only one.

"That's kind of why I'm here," she mumbled.

Cassie's eyes brightened. "You're getting married?"

"Nee, but I want to—I mean, I think I'm going to see the matchmaker."

Cassie waggled her eyebrows. "What about Luke? I always thought you'd marry him!"

"He's the one I'm going to see her about," Lettie said. "He's gone to her and asked her to get him a *fraa* because his niece and nephew need a *mudder*. He's their guardian now that his *brudder* passed away."

"How did you find all that out?"

"He told me," Lettie sat down with Simon, who was beginning to get heavy. "He was at the school today because the matchmaker sent him over there to fix the window before it gets too cold."

"Why would he tell you all that unless he wanted you to know for some reason?" Cassie asked. "But what would be his reason for you to know unless he was planning on asking you? Do you think he was fishing to see how you'd react? Or maybe he said it to make you jealous!"

Lettie shook his head. "I think we're too old for those kinds of games, but I agree it doesn't make sense that he felt the need to tell me. He didn't ask me to take a buggy ride if that's what you're thinking. But he did ask me to help him with his nephew, Eli. The boy is having trouble in school."

"That could throw the two of you together a lot," Cassie commented with a big smile. "You should take him and the *kinner* some supper!"

Lettie scowled. "That again? We've been over this a million times; if I take supper to him, he'll invite me to stay out of obligation, and I want him to invite because he wants to date me, not because I'm throwing myself at him; with supper in my hands! You've been trying to get me to take food to him for more than a month since the funeral, and it's just not something I feel comfortable doing."

"Don't you get it?" Cassie asked. "This is your chance. Take him a meal and let him know you're interested in becoming his *fraa.*"

"Ach, what if I'm not?"

Cassie smirked, rolling her fiery green eyes at her friend. "We both know that isn't true; you have been in love with Luke for as long as I can remember, and that is why you'd rather be a spinster than marry anyone but him!"

Lettie bit her bottom lip; sometimes, it was irritating that her friend knew her so well.

"What am I going to do?" Lettie asked. "Do you think I should go to the matchmaker and ask her to set me up with Luke? Having Miss Sadie put us together is less brazen than what you're suggesting!"

"You could be a coward and do it that way, or you could take Luke some supper and get yourself an invitation to partake in the meal with him and the *kinner;* that way you can show him how you interact with them outside of your classroom."

"I don't know if I can be that bold," Lettie admitted.

"Do you want to take care of other people's *kinner* all day for the rest of your life, or do you want some of your own?" Cassie asked her. "He wants a *fraa,* and I *know* you don't want to be teaching *his* and his *fraa's kinner* in a few years!"

Lettie shuddered; the very thought of it made her sick to her stomach.

"You know what a chicken I am," she complained. "What if I go over there and take supper to Luke and he *doesn't* invite me to stay? Do you have any idea how embarrassed I'd be?"

Cassie blew out a breath. "I know you'd probably want to crawl under a rock, but if it turned out that way, at least you'd know how he felt once and for all. You've been wondering if he liked you for more years than I can count. Take a chance; what have you got to lose?"

"My dignity!"

Cassie shook her head. "You're thinking about this all wrong; take him supper and get yourself a husband and a couple of *kinner;* I know you like the twins, so what's the problem?"

Lettie bounced Simon and smiled at him, a lump forming in her throat. "I want my own *kinner;* you know that, but Luke gets under my skin. I have kind of a love-hate thing going for him!"

"Stop thinking of all the tricks he played on you when you were in school," Cassie advised. "See him for who he is now; he's an adult, and he's handsome and needs a *fraa*. What more of a sign do you need? I can whack you on the head with a log if that's what it'll take to knock some sense into you!"

"Ach, when you put it that way, it seems easy," Lettie said. "But he gets my stomach all in knots every time I see him."

"That's called love, Lettie!"

Could it be that easy?

"What if he doesn't want me?"

"Do you remember how insecure I was about Ben?" Cassie reminded her. "You have to push past it and tell him how you feel—even if you can't say it with words. Say it with food; no *mann* can turn down food—especially the way you cook!"

Cassie was right about that; if there was one place where Lettie was at her most confident, it was in the kitchen.

CHAPTER FOUR

Lettie's mouth fell open when she answered the door; Jordan Yoder was the last person she would have expected to see showing up on her father's doorstep. Her parents had left for the summer to go to her sister's house to help with the birth of her fourth child and hadn't returned yet. She'd made a trip to visit the new arrival just before school had started, but her parents were content to stay there another few weeks. Lettie was sure that if Jordan knew her father was home, he'd have never had the guts to show up; everyone in the community knew her father was famous for running off potential suitors for his youngest daughter. The only way her older sister, Annie, had been lucky enough to marry was because she ran off to another community and got married behind their parents' backs. Lettie suspected if the opportunity ever arose for her to marry, she'd have to do the same as Annie had. Run away—as far as possible!

With her mother away all summer, Lettie had been able to have some freedoms, but hadn't taken advantage of them the way she'd wanted to. She'd prayed for a man to come around asking to take her for a buggy ride, but the offer hadn't presented itself. Was that the reason for Jordan's visit?

"Hello, Jordan," she said, remembering her manners.

He removed his black hat and cleared his throat. "I know it's short notice, but I was wondering if you'd like to go for a buggy ride with me this evening."

Lettie bit her bottom lip to keep from laughing; was this really happening? She'd spent the entire afternoon making food and was about to take it to Luke. How was she going to get out of this predicament?

She cleared her throat and looked him in the eye. "I was about to hitch my pony cart to take a meal over to the King *familye,*" she said, hoping he'd take the hint.

Cassie had sent her home earlier with some fresh vegetables that her husband, Ben, was growing in his hydroponic greenhouse, and Lettie was excited to use them in the supper she was making for Luke and the children.

"I'd be happy to take you by there to drop off the supper—and then we could take that buggy ride," he said with a smile. "If you want to."

He wasn't a bad-looking young man, but he was at least five years younger than she was, and they would not make a good match because of it. That, and he wasn't the man she wanted—Luke was the man she'd pined over since grade-school. Having Jordan tagging along when she took the meal over to Luke would not get her an invitation to supper; that was the whole purpose of her taking the meal over, wasn't it?

She sighed inwardly.

No, the purpose was to take a meal over to a grieving family, and that was that. She'd have to visit the matchmaker for the rest of it. She would have to be mature and put her personal desires aside for the night and go along with whatever reason Jordan was here. Everything had a purpose, didn't it?

Lettie pasted on a smile. *"Danki,* I would appreciate that."

Perhaps if Luke saw her taking a buggy ride with another man, it might light a fire under him to ask her for a buggy ride. She wasn't the type of woman to play games and try to make a man jealous, but maybe he thought she wasn't interested in getting married—being the schoolteacher and all. Perhaps that was the reason he hadn't asked her. But she prayed that being with Jordan would, at the very least, remind Luke that she was available. At least she hoped so.

Lettie opened the door to Jordan and invited him in.

"I hope you don't mind that the matchmaker suggested I ask you for a buggy ride," Jordan said as he followed her into the kitchen.

Lettie spun on her heels to face him. "The matchmaker sent you here?"

He nodded and gulped. "That's alright, isn't it?"

Lettie pasted her smile back on. "I'm just surprised, that's all—mostly since I hadn't gone to her myself to ask for a match."

Why would the matchmaker suggest Jordan match up with me unless she was up to something? Unless Cassie talked to her before she got a chance to.

Cassie and Miss Sadie were close neighbors, and she could easily have mentioned something to the woman; both ladies were busybodies when it came to matters of the heart, but in a good way. Lettie wasn't sure how she felt about being experimented on in this way, but there must be a reason for it, and she would not know unless she played along.

"I'm sorry if my being here tonight is an intrusion, but Miss Sadie was particular about having me pay you a visit tonight," he said, clamping a hand over his mouth. "*Ach,* I wasn't supposed to tell you that."

What are those two up to?

Lettie glared at him, using her best *teacher* look. "Was there anything else you weren't supposed to tell me?"

Jordan shrugged. "Only that she thought you might like some help taking food over to the King's *haus* tonight."

So that was it; Cassie told the matchmaker she was taking supper over to Luke, and her well-meaning friend thought it would be good to take along some *husband insurance*, and poor Jordan was it. Well, he was more like bait to hook herself a husband.

"I could use some help," she admitted. "It seems I made enough for the whole community, but I wanted to make sure they had plenty of leftovers for school lunches for the *kinner.*"

"That was very kind of you," he said. "What can I help with?"

She'd spent the entire afternoon baking bread and biscuits and a few batches of cookies as well as two pies. She did that on top of cooking a large batch of fried chicken, about ten potatoes, and she'd even made a fresh green salad with lots of tomatoes, cucumbers, and carrots from Ben's hydroponic garden.

With another pair of hands, Lettie would have all of it packed in no time at all.

Jordan's eyes popped when she pointed out all that she would be taking with her to the family. She was trying to make a good impression, but she might have gone a little overboard. No worries; they would have plenty to last them at least over the weekend and into the first part of the week. At least she prayed it was so; she had no idea how much children could eat, but she remembered her father complaining when her brother became a teenager. Seven years old wasn't quite a teen, but she'd seen Eli put away a lot of food at lunchtime, and she wanted to be prepared. To send too little food to the family would be more of an embarrassment than too much, and before Jordan showed up, she was hoping for an invitation to share some of it with them. Second-guessing herself, she thought she better leave a couple of rolls and a few pieces of the chicken behind so she could eat later once she returned from the impromptu buggy ride with him. She prayed that things would take a turn, and she wouldn't have to take the buggy ride with him; they had nothing in common with the guy, and she wasn't interested.

Lettie gave Jordan the go-ahead to put the baked items on the table in his buggy while she finished packaging up the mashed potatoes and gravy into plastic containers with lids. She'd put the fried chicken into a glass dish with a lid and zipped it up in an insulated cover to keep it warm. The rest was ready to go. She'd put the baked goods except for the pies in plastic baggies, but she'd used up every piece of Tupperware in her mother's kitchen packing the rest of the food for them, and she prayed Luke was good at getting those items back to the women in the community who'd been taking food over to them.

When all the food was packed, Lettie hesitated before allowing Jordan to assist her into his open buggy; once she was seated, she said a little prayer that no one would see them together and get the wrong impression.

****

Luke was in the middle of washing up for supper when a knock sounded at the door. He'd grown used to having meals delivered to him from the women in the community, and he would almost mourn the loss of them once they stopped. He prayed he'd have a wife by then, but as tongue-tied as he got every time he was around Lettie, he feared he would have to accept the match that Miss Sadie would find for him instead of the only woman that would fill the gap in his heart.

He dried his hands and turned around toward a young voice and looked into a pair of green eyes belonging to Annabelle Bontrager; up until now, all the women who'd paid him a visit with meals had been married or widowed. Annabelle was young and single—and Lettie's cousin.

She smiled at Luke, and it made him a little nervous. "The matchmaker suggested I bring over a meal for you," Annabelle said with a flirtatious tone.

Luke gulped. "The matchmaker?" he asked, his voice cracking.

Was Annabelle the woman that Miss Sadie decided should be his match? Was it too late to take back his request?

"Jah, she said you were looking for a match when I went over to see her today for the same reason, and she sent me here to see if you'd like to have supper with me!"

Luke pursed his lips; Annabelle was at least five or six years younger than he was, and in his opinion, too young to be mothering the twins. She was only a little more than twice their age, and he didn't think she was qualified. Besides, being that young, she'd want *kinner* of her own, and he wasn't ready for that yet with the instant responsibility of his niece and nephew. He'd been around them since they were born and had even helped raise them since his brother's wife had passed away giving birth to the twins. It wasn't as if he hadn't been a second parent to them all their lives, but things would be different with a wife.

He didn't see Annabelle as being up for the task of keeping his wayward nephew in check. That, and he just wasn't attracted to her in any way—emotional or physical, despite her being quite pretty.

Still, she was here, and the food she'd brought smelled good enough to make his stomach growl, but he didn't trust her not to be up to something. He'd rather have to eat leftovers or make supper himself than to keep her company under the guise of courting her. If he didn't reject her advances now, it would be too late later because it would only cause misunderstandings.

"*Danki* for bringing supper to me, but…"

He was about to send her and her food away when an approaching buggy interrupted him.

Perhaps it was one of the other women in the community coming to rescue him from being forced into an unplanned dinner date with Annabelle.

"Miss Fisher is here!" Eli gushed.

At least he likes his teacher even though he can't seem to behave for her, Luke thought.

He had to admit; he was happy she was here too; it would give him an excuse to send Annabelle on her way.

Luke opened the door, his eyes wide at his unexpected guests. Lettie had come with young Jordan Yoder; they unpacked food from his buggy and brought it to the door.

Luke pasted on a smile, wondering what he was going to do with so many dinner guests. Should he invite them all and hope the evening would fix itself in the right direction, or did he dare be unhospitable to Annabelle and Jordan? No, he couldn't send two away for the sake of one—could he?

"I brought enough food to feed the entire community," Lettie said, eyeing Annabelle. "How many are here?"

"Only me!" Annabelle said with a nasty tone that Luke didn't care to hear. "I came here with supper and a proposal for Luke."

Lettie raised her eyebrows and stared at Luke.

Luke turned back to Annabelle. "I started to tell you a few minutes ago," he said with a shaky voice. "Lettie and I already had a supper engagement."

"What about Jordan?" Annabelle complained, pointing to Lettie's tagalong.

"He gave me and all the food a ride over here," Lettie offered. "I'm sure he'd be happy to take you home."

Luke tried not to smile; was Lettie just as eager to be rid of her supper companion as he was to get rid of his? If so, he'd play along if it meant getting rid of the whiny Annabelle.

Annabelle scowled. "I brought my own buggy, and I planned to have supper with you, Luke, because the matchmaker sent me over here after telling me you were looking for a *fraa.*"

Luke's heart hiccupped just before speeding out of control.

"But I already found myself a *fraa,*" he said, flashing Lettie a pleading look.

Annabelle scrunched up her face. "My cousin, the school-teacher? But she's a spinster! Why would you want to marry her?"

Do you want the long list of reasons? Luke started to chuckle but coughed to cover it up.

"She won't be a spinster once we're married."

"You're marrying Miss Fisher?" Ellie gushed, throwing herself into Lettie's arms. "I'm so happy you're going to be *mei mamm!*"

Eli did the same, and Lettie pulled them both into a hug. She flashed Luke a weak smile, but he couldn't help either of them out of this jam; his foot was wedged so far in his mouth, it was nearly choking him to death.

CHAPTER FIVE

Lettie's cheeks warmed at Luke's comment; had he meant he wanted to marry her, or was he merely trying to get out of a jam with Annabelle? She didn't imagine him being interested in her whiny, immature cousin who was five years too young for him, but who was she to judge? She'd shown up at his house with Jordan in tow, but she hadn't missed the mischievous smile on Luke's face when she suggested that Jordan take Annabelle home for him. For that look alone, a red flag went up in her mind, and it made her wonder if she could trust him not to act like the old Luke from their school days. He was up to something, but she had a feeling Annabelle and Jordan were too. The only difference between Annabelle's something and Jordan's something was that Lettie knew her cousin would have her own agenda with Luke, and Jordan didn't appear to have any designs on her in the least.

The biggest problems with this situation were the twins, who were grappling onto her as if they were drowning in the lake, and she was a life preserver. The twins certainly wanted her for their mother, but did Luke honestly want her for a wife, or was it all an act to get rid of her cousin?

Annabelle packed up her food with a huff and began to walk out when Jordan offered to help her carry it out of the King's home. Before he left, he turned around and nodded her direction.

"I'm sorry for the intrusion; if I'd known you were already betrothed, I wouldn't have asked you for a buggy ride," Jordan said.

Luke slapped him on the back with a friendly smile. "No harm done; you didn't know."

Luke closed the door behind them after apologizing for the *misunderstanding*.

Ach, that was no misunderstanding, Lettie thought as he closed the door, his smile unfading. *That was pure sabotage by the matchmaker, and instead of Jordan being bait for Luke, I turned out to be the bait.*

Luke turned around to face her; what could he say to her with the twins bouncing on their heels, asking when the wedding was going to be. His look turned from a satisfied smile to a nervous twitch of a smile, but Lettie ignored him.

"Miss Fisher and I have to discuss this, but it's not for sure yet, so don't get your hopes up."

Was he trying to worm his way out of it? Lettie didn't think it would matter at this point because the twins were not going to let him off the hook that easily; should she?

"But, you love her!" Ellie blurted out with a sing-song voice. "I heard you tell *mei dat* just before he went to heaven!"

Luke dropped his gaze to the young girl and chuckled, though his cheeks turned red. Lettie bit her bottom lip to keep from reacting, but her heart pounded in her ears. Did Luke really say such a thing to his brother?

"You should know better than to eavesdrop on adult conversations, and you shouldn't repeat things you heard from a private conversation," Luke reprimanded her.

"I'm sorry, *Onkel* Luke,"

His cheeks were aflame, and Lettie almost felt sorry for the predicament the twins were putting him in. If not for that one pesky little problem she had, she wanted to marry him, and she wasn't so sure if he felt the same way.

Ellie bounced on her heels in front of Lettie, looking up at her with big blue, hopeful eyes. "Please tell *Onkel* Luke you'll marry him; we want you to be our *mudder.*"

"*Jah,*" Eli chimed in. "We never had a *mudder,* and we need one!"

This was not what she'd expected when she decided to take a meal over to Luke and the children; she never thought in a million years she'd be about to accept a proposal from two of her students on behalf of their uncle, but she couldn't resist.

"That's not a conversation for *kinner*," she scolded them.

They threw themselves at Luke. "Ask her, *Onkel* Luke," they begged. "Ask her to be our *mudder.*"

They weren't asking him to propose marriage; they were asking him to offer *motherhood*. Did she want that? She unquestionably adored the twins, but they were asking for a lifetime commitment, not a few hours a day in her classroom.

It was time to let him off the hook and keep herself from embarrassment; it was evident to her he wasn't ready to propose to her, but if she were to marry him, she'd have to do it quickly before her father returned from Annie's house.

"Why don't we sit down and eat our supper before it gets cold," Lettie said, shooing the children toward the table.

They groaned but obeyed her.

"I brought cookies and pie," she said, enjoying the spark that returned to their eyes. "If we don't eat supper, how are you going to get to the dessert?"

Luke agreed after flashing her a look; was it gratitude in his eyes or something else?

Both children hurried to do as they were told while Lettie took charge as if it were her classroom, giving orders to get dishes and doling out the food. She served the children first and then Luke, and afterward, she helped herself. Her stomach was growling, and she was interested in seeing where the evening would take them. With her stomach all full of butterflies, would she be able to finish her meal?

****

Luke sat across from Lettie, watching and listening while she conversed with the twins. They liked her a lot, and that pleased him; they loved her enough to want her to be their mother. His heart pounded wildly at the prospect of marrying Lettie. It had been what he'd wanted for a lot of years, so why did the reality of it make him so nervous? He couldn't tell for sure, but she wasn't as enthusiastic as he was, and he worried she wasn't on board with the idea of marrying him. She was a tough one to read; even her expressions were beyond his suspicions. She was smart and beautiful; she was the whole package, but he'd not been very kind to her when they were in school. He'd never forget the last time he ever teased her; he'd made her cry, and it had nearly broken his heart. He knew better than to put the plastic spider on her sweater, but he'd done it anyway. She'd screamed and tried to peel off her sweater; in the struggle, she'd tripped over the woodpile behind the school and broken her arm. Every day while her arm healed, he'd offered to carry her things to school, but every day she refused him. Had she finally forgiven him, or would he forever have to pay for that dumb prank?

Then it hit him; that might be the answer to getting Eli to focus on his studies and stop being such a goof-off at school. If he shared that story with the boy and let him see that his own shenanigans had hurt his teacher, he might just stop. Maybe he could compare his actions and tell him that, in a way, he was hurting his teacher too by constantly disrupting her class. Eli cared for her, and if he could convey it in a way that wouldn't cause the boy to feel guilt, perhaps it might work. The last thing he wanted was for his nephew to have to live with the kind of guilt he'd had to live with all these years for causing Lettie to break her arm when they were younger.

After the silent prayer, Luke dipped one of his biscuits in the mountain of mashed potatoes and gravy and sank his teeth into the warm, buttery treat. He hadn't had biscuits this good since his mother had baked a batch. Next, he bit into the fried chicken and closed his eyes against its goodness. If he didn't know better, he'd have to wonder if his mother had paid a heavenly visit and made this meal. He was always first in line for Lettie's fried chicken and biscuits at the meals after church, but having them in his own home felt like a sign that she was meant to be here with the generous meal she'd made for him and the children.

"*Danki* for blessing us with this delicious meal," he said when silence fell on the room.

She looked up at him and smiled, gave him a nod, and then went back to her meal.

Was she being polite for the children's sake, or was she waiting for his answer? He didn't want to propose to her simply because the children insisted; he wanted to give her a genuine proposal, and he wanted a straightforward answer from her. He didn't want to spend his life wondering if she'd said yes to him because she'd felt obligated not to hurt the children's feelings. He wanted her love, and for that, he would have to prove to her that he was no longer that same boy who'd caused her to break her arm. He prayed she would take him seriously when the time came for him to propose, but today was not that day. He wanted to court her properly; the last thing he would do was rush her into deciding out of pity or obligation to him or the children.

When they finished their meal, the children rushed up behind Lettie and were bouncing on their heels before she had a chance to slice the pecan pie. She handed two slices to each child and asked them to put them on the table; once she covered the pie, she was back at the table, but the twins had nearly finished.

"I'm happy to see you like the pie so much!" Lettie said with a smile.

Eli put his fork down and chewed his mouthful as if he was in the running for first place in a pie-eating contest. He swallowed and turned toward his uncle. "Will you answer the question now?" he begged.

Luke gulped; the kid had a one-track mind.

"Why don't we talk about our plans for the fall picnic tomorrow," Luke suggested, aiming the conversation more to Lettie than to the children. "Would you like to go along with us, Miss Fisher?"

The children bolted from their chairs and rushed to each side of her, staring at her as if their lives depended on her agreeing to share their Saturday afternoon plans.

She glanced at Luke, looking for approval and he nodded, hoping she'd agree.

"*Jah,* I'd like to go along with you," she said with a smile. "*Danki,* for inviting me."

Luke's heart sped up; was she going to make this easy on him? He prayed she would.

"If you're going with us, does that mean you're courting us?" Eli asked with an innocence that even Luke couldn't get upset with.

Lettie drew her hand toward her mouth, and Luke could see she was trying to hide a smile. "We can talk about that *after* we've had a chance to get to know each other."

"But we know you, Miss Fisher," Ellie said. "We see you every day at school, and you take real *gut* care of all the *kinner,* so we know you'll make a *gut mudder.*"

"*Ach,* why don't we give Miss Fisher some space," Luke said with a firm voice.

Lettie rose from her chair and began to clear the table, but Luke stopped her. "We can clean things up; you're our guest."

She smiled. *"Nee,* it seems I've become an honorary member of the *familye."*

Her comment brought heat to his cheeks and stirred up the butterflies in his stomach.

Lettie continued to clear the table, and Ellie started filling the sink with sudsy water to wash the dishes. "I'm going to help you, so you'll know what a *gut* girl I am. Maybe then you'll want to be *mei mudder* if you see how *gut* I can wash the dishes."

Luke could see by the kindness in Lettie's eyes she didn't have the heart to turn away Ellie's help. It pleased him to see Ellie wanting to be a helper instead of trying to do it all on her own the way she had been since her father became ill. When he passed on, she threw herself into every chore, taking on a grownup motherly role, and Luke was determined to give her back her childhood if he had to hogtie Lettie and beg her to be his wife.

"I'll come in and check on you in a bit to see when I should hitch up the team," he said. "Since Jordan left with Annabelle, I'm guessing you're going to need a ride home."

Lettie smiled with downcast eyes. He could see she'd forgotten about that little detail, but he surely hadn't; he was looking forward to taking her home even if it wasn't an official buggy ride.

CHAPTER SIX

Lettie finished putting away the last of the dishes and sent Ellie outside to let Luke know she was ready to go. Ellie had chatted her ear off the entire time they washed the dishes, telling her all the things they could do once she was her mother. Honestly, it would have filled Lettie with excitement if she wasn't so worried that Luke wasn't as eager for her to become part of the family as the children were. Though he acted as if he was on board with the idea of marrying her, there was a part of him that expressed reservation. He'd kept trying to divert the twins' attention away from the subject, and she had to wonder why.

The question remained as to why he'd said it in the first place. If it was only to get rid of her cousin: that was a cruel trick to play on her and the children whose hearts were fully vested in the idea of having her for a mother. If getting rid of Annabelle had been his only driving force for the back-handed proposal, he'd be in for dealing with the twins' heartache once he took it back—not to mention her broken heart. She didn't know whether to feel embarrassed that he kept changing the subject, or to be relieved that he was not pushing her on the issue.

Lettie dried her hands and soaked in the quaint, red and white kitchen, thinking about how nice it would be to have such a large kitchen to do her baking. Her mother's kitchen was so tiny; she had no idea how her mother had managed all those years. What with raising three children and always helping with the community bake sales, it was a wonder her mother survived it all those years. Yes, a kitchen this large would be nice, but not if it came with a marriage of convenience.

Am I really daydreaming about Luke's kitchen? Most women would be dreaming about the mann, wouldn't they?

The trouble with Lettie daydreaming about Luke was that she still held a bit of a grudge against him for being so mean to her all those years in school. All the teasing and laughing at her expense, not to mention her broken arm. Maybe it was time to let that go. He was not the same troublemaking, mouthy boy any more than she was that same awkward *smarty-pants* as he'd referred to her too often. She was still smart, and bookworm, but maybe he was mature enough finally to appreciate those qualities in her.

Ach, who am I kidding? He still sees me as that little girl in her own world, and he just played the ultimate trick on her—didn't he? Lying about her being his betrothed was far worse than causing her to break her arm!

So, why couldn't she seem to get past that? Did she fear more tricks from him, or was it a matter of learning to trust the man he was now that they were grown-up? How could she trust him when he'd just lied about the two of them being betrothed?

Either way, something was holding her back, but it wasn't his looks. She was very attracted to him, but there had to be more to it than a physical attraction for things to work out between them. They needed a good foundation to build on, and that would have to start with trust.

Eli came bounding in the kitchen, out of breath. "Are you going to leave the cookies and the pie here for us?"

Lettie smiled at the boy. "Of course I will; I brought them here to give them to you."

"Will you make more for us when you come back to stay when you become our *mudder?*" Eli asked.

How was Luke going to talk his way out of this? How was she?

Lettie stared at the boy, whose smile was so full of hope, she knew she had to choose her words wisely, so she didn't hurt his feelings. "I'm not sure when I'll be back," she tried to say. "Or if I will, but I suppose that's up to your *Onkel* Luke."

Eli's face drew back in a frown. "Don't you want to be our *mudder?*"

Lettie looked down into his innocent eyes, and she wanted to cry. "It's a little more complicated than what I want or don't want. Your *Onkel* Luke and I have a few things to work out between us before we can think about being a *familye.*"

"*Ach,* is it because he broke your arm when you were *kinner?*"

Lettie's breath hitched. "He told you about that?"

"*Jah,* he told me that when I act up in your class, it hurts you the same way he used to hurt you," Eli said with downcast eyes.

"*Nee,* that's not true!" Lettie said, fuming that Luke would say such a thing to the boy. "It's not the same at all. It doesn't hurt me, but it makes me think you don't like school."

80

Eli looked up at her with wide eyes. "So, it doesn't hurt you?"

Lettie hadn't thought about the similarities, and she supposed now she understood why Luke might have shared the stories with the boy.

"Not in the same way, but I suppose it does hurt a little," she admitted.

"I'm sorry," he said.

She patted his head and smiled. "I don't think you do it on purpose."

Not the way Luke did, anyway.

The question was, did it hurt more coming from Luke's nephew more than it would any other student? Perhaps, but she couldn't fault Eli for that. Was she holding him accountable for what Luke did so many years ago? Maybe not, but perhaps she was pooling him in with the old version of Luke, and that wasn't fair to Eli. He hadn't been a bad student for his first two years with her; it was only this year that he was acting up. The only thing that had changed was having his father pass away just before they began school, which led her back to her original worry that maybe they shouldn't have started school so soon. Maybe Eli needed more time to mourn even though both children were grieving in their own way. Eli, with his antics and Ellie, with her sudden quiet and withdrawn personality.

"I better get back outside and help *Onkel* Luke hitch up the horse," Eli said.

Not long after, Ellie popped her head inside the kitchen door to let her know Luke was waiting outside with the buggy. Lettie hung up the dish towel and swept her gaze around the kitchen to be sure she didn't miss anything. Everything was clean and put away—especially her heart, which she suddenly felt as if she were leaving it behind in the red and white kitchen with the family that might never be hers.

She exited the house in time to see Luke helping Ellie into the back of the family buggy with Eli. He extended a hand to her to assist her, and she took it though it was awkward. The warmth from his hand caused her heart to flutter, and her cheeks heated up, but she was too afraid to allow herself to enjoy the spark that flickered between them. Once everyone was settled, he sat beside her on the front bench and set the horse in motion.

Was this what it was like to have a family? She let her gaze follow Luke and then to the back where the twins were leaning against each other and already falling asleep; they'd had a long day. By the time they reached her farm, Lettie had spent the entire time distracted almost to the point of allowing her desire for the handsome farmer to rid her of her senses. His knee had continuously knocked into hers the whole way there, and she could not concentrate on anything besides the warmth it put in her cheeks.

Luke hopped down from the buggy and assisted her out; his warm hand sent tingles down her spine and caused her lashes to flutter at the closeness between them when her feet touched the ground. He cleared his throat and walked beside her to her door, neither of them speaking. But once she reached her destination, she turned to thank him and bid him goodnight but couldn't find her voice.

"I'm sorry about the pressure the twins put on you tonight," he said, lowering his head. "The truth is, they do need a *mudder,* and I know I'm not the ideal *mann* in your eyes, but they seem to have their hearts set on you—if you'll just think about it—for their sake." Then he added, "I'll pick you up at ten o'clock tomorrow for the picnic."

Lettie bit her bottom lip and nodded; it wasn't a proposal, only a suggestion. Did he intend to propose? If not, they would never be able to marry; once her father returned to the community, he'd object, and that would be her last chance to avoid spinsterhood.

Luke left the porch and ran out to his buggy, and she let herself inside her empty house. Once she was safe inside, she put her back to the door and allowed her emotion to take over. Tears spilled from her eyes, and anger welled up from her gut. Part of her was insulted by his lack of proposal, and the other part was humiliated that her only worth in the man's eyes was as a mother to his niece and nephew. How was she supposed to get through a picnic with him tomorrow when he was only interested in her as a mother for the twins?

****

Luke chided himself all the way home for the way he'd presented his proposal to Lettie—if he could even call it that; she deserved better from him than a backhanded proposal to be the twins' mother. He'd acted like the biggest coward a man could be. Why was he always so tongue-tied around that woman? Perhaps because her soft brown eyes burrowed a hole right through him every time he was around her, and it made him feel like that little boy who broke her arm so many years ago.

Had she forgiven him for that, or would it always be between them? Perhaps tomorrow, he could find a way to make it up to her. He didn't lack for attraction toward her, but that wasn't enough for a woman like her. He'd always cared for her and even had a secret crush on her when they were young, but maybe it was time he grew up and showed her how he felt about her without the childhood antics that never got him anywhere with her besides provoking contempt in her heart for him.

Lord, show me the way to Lettie's heart; I don't want to marry any other woman besides her. I realized that when Annabelle showed up at my haus with food, but when Lettie showed up too, I'd never been so happy to see her in all my life! Help me to make up for the past, if necessary, and help me to show her how much I've always cared for her. Help me to tame my tongue when I'm around her, so I won't insult her the way I used to when we were kinner.

Danki, Amen.

When he returned home, he tucked the twins into bed and began their prayers with them. It nearly broke his heart when they included Lettie in their prayers and asked God to make her their mother. He couldn't help but include the same prayer for himself but for her to be his wife.

****

Lettie couldn't stop thinking about Luke; could they survive a marriage of convenience? And what of his strong

86

personality? Would she be able to live with *two* tricksters? Between Luke and his nephew, she wasn't sure if she could tame either of them, but if she were to accept Luke's backhanded proposal, she would do her best to try.

She'd tossed and turned most of the night, excitement and disappointment playing tug-of-war with her heartstrings. How would she keep her emotions in check around Luke when he'd made it clear he only wanted a mother for the twins? If he'd expressed a genuine interest in the marriage itself, she would not feel so torn between accepting or rejecting his offer. Thinking back on it, the proposal had been more the twins' idea, even though he'd been the one to announce he needed a wife. His only *need* for a wife was to have a mother for the children. Did he believe her to be the best candidate for the position, or had he merely extended that offer to her because the children had insisted and put so much pressure on him?

Her thoughts were tainted with grief as she went about her morning chores, but she pushed down the emotion to keep her mind on task; she planned to be ready by the time Luke and the children arrived for the picnic. She was eager to spend some time with them and hoped things would be different outside the classroom—for Luke and the twins. If they didn't have such a strained history, she might not feel so nervous. Had it been God's will for her to be at his house last night at the same time as Annabelle, or had it been the musings of the matchmaker to sabotage his dinner plans? She believed Miss Sadie was behind both their surprise dinner companions and being the wise older woman she was; she had to have known precisely how the evening would pan out. Had the woman planned it that way or had she and Luke been pawns in her matchmaking schemes?

Only time would tell.

CHAPTER SEVEN

Lettie's heart sped up when buggy wheels grinding in her driveway, pricked her ears. She'd baked a batch of cookies and made a ham and macaroni casserole to take with them to the picnic

They arrive at the Bishop's house on the lake for the picnic, and all eyes were on them. Embarrassment filled Lettie's cheeks with heat, but the twins were soaking it up.

Luke parked the buggy and helped Lettie down, and then scooped up Ellie and lifted her out of the buggy.

The Bishop walked over to greet them. "I'm so glad to see you've made a match," he said, looking between Lettie and Luke with a smile.

Lettie opened her mouth to correct him, but the twins each grabbed one of her hands.

"She's going to be our new *mudder,*" Ellie said with such a sweet and innocent voice that Lettie didn't have the heart to correct her.

Instead, she turned to Luke, who smiled, his chest slightly puffed as he walked away with the Bishop to discuss the wedding plans he hadn't even discussed with her yet.

What just happened?

Here she stood with a child's hand in each of hers, realizing she already fit into the role as their mother. What would the parents of her other students think if they saw her? Would the news of their supposed engagement get around to everyone who'd gathered for the picnic faster than she could get herself a plate of food? Was she expected to tote around the twins all day alone as their new *mother,* or was Luke coming back for them? She'd arrived with Luke, so they would all assume he was courting her, wouldn't they? She suddenly felt a little queasy, and she had to sit down.

Lettie migrated toward a bench under an oak tree in the yard while the children followed. Of course, they followed; they still clung to her hands as if they belonged to her, and she practically dragged them along with her to the bench.

"I'm glad you're going to marry *Onkel* Luke, and I'm glad you'll be our *mudder*," Eli said with an innocent smile.

"Why do you think I'm going to get married to your *Onkel* Luke?" Lettie asked him.

"Because he promised our *dat* he would marry you so you could be our *mudder*," Eli answered.

More eavesdropping! Lettie thought to herself. *Surely, Eli wasn't making this up; kinner can't make up stuff like that, can they?*

"I think you should let the deciding be up to the adults, Eli," Lettie said, her tone firm.

Ellie looked up at her with doe eyes. "Please marry him; I want a *mamm* to help me cook and clean the *haus.*"

"*Ach,* you do all that now on your own?" Lettie asked.

"*Jah,*" she said. "Except for supper because someone brings it for us, but *Onkel* Luke said they probably won't bring supper to us anymore since it's been a month now since *Dat* went to heaven."

Lettie sighed. So that was Luke's hurry to get married; he was about to have to cook and clean and be a mother to the twins if he didn't get himself a wife soon.

"Will the two of you please get the food from the buggy and take it to the table with the rest of the food?" Lettie asked, standing and testing her wobbly legs. She was still a little shaky, but she couldn't sit under the tree all day as if she were waiting for Luke to come back and fetch her. She needed to find Cassie for some much-needed girl-talk.

****

Lettie spotted Cassie getting out of her buggy with her husband and *kinner,* figuring she'd give her a few minutes to join the other picnickers before bombarding her with her troubles. Before she could approach her, Luke caught up to her.

"Where did the twins run off to?" he asked her.

She pointed to them over at the dessert table; she'd been keeping an eye on them, ready to step in if they should help themselves to the sweets before the Bishop gathered everyone for the prayer over the meal. She wasn't sure why it concerned her so much that they eat some supper before they delved into the sweets, but she suspected some maternal instincts were trying to kick in.

"Should I get them away from the sugary treats before they're tempted to ruin their supper?" he asked Lettie as if it was partly her decision what the twins did.

She shook her head. "I've been watching to make sure they didn't get their hands into everything, and so far, they've just been eyeing everything."

"*Jah,* but *kinner* can only handle the temptation for so long before they get themselves into trouble," Luke said with a chuckle.

"*Jah,* but you have to give them a little slack to show you trust them too," Lettie advised him. "If you don't, they will always depend on you to make the decisions for them. This way, you let them learn a little self-control."

"I can see you're going to be able to make a bigger difference with Eli in your classroom," Luke said, watching the twins.

"What do you mean?"

"I think Eli will behave better in class if you're his *mudder* and his teacher. You'll have the authority to discipline him, and he needs that."

"That's an unfair spot to put me in," Lettie fumed.

"I'm not the one who put you on the spot; the twins did that. They want you to be their *mudder,* and I think it will fix a lot of things—including the behavior problem in your class," Luke said. "The Bishop said he could marry us Wednesday after school lets out, so I can pick you up and we can ride together. We can move your things after the ceremony."

"I didn't say I was going to marry you," Lettie said with a stiff upper lip.

"You didn't object, so I assumed you were onboard." Luke retorted.

"I might have been if you'd proposed to me, but you never asked."

Luke chuckled. "Don't tell me you're one of *those girls!*"

Lettie's lips formed a thin line, and her eyes narrowed. "What do you mean by *one of those girls?*"

He straightened up his smile and cleared his throat. "You know—the kind who needs a formal proposal."

"To be *asked* at all would be nice; it's proper to do so."

"Well, I'm sorry if I don't know how to talk to you—you always were sort of *difficult* to approach," Luke said.

Lettie sucked in her breath. "Difficult? You think *I'm* difficult?"

He forced a smile. "You don't think I'm the difficult one, do you?"

Lettie took a moment before answering; this was good, wasn't it? They were getting everything out in the open, but she was not about to allow his insults to go much longer. Should she put him in his place or take the high road? Why couldn't he just propose instead of hiding behind the children? Should she agree only to keep from having her father object to the marriage? Surely, once she got married, he would not be able to do anything about it—same as with Annie.

"Maybe if you didn't have your nose stuffed in a book all the time," Luke interrupted her thoughts. "You might see the world around you for what it is!"

Lettie drew in a breath and let the fire from her gut come out in flames. "I think I see things just as they are, and I can see that you haven't changed one bit since we were *kinner!*"

"You can see me however you want to, but I wish you could open your eyes and see that I'm trying the best I can to live up to *mei brudder's* last wishes, but I need *a fraa* and a *mudder* for his *kinner,* and for some reason they seem to want *you* for their *mudder!*" Luke said. "So you're either going to have to agree to marry me, or *you* can be the one to break the bad news to them."

Lettie sucked in her breath. "I'm sorry for your loss, but I did not ask you to me in the middle of your *familye* crisis, and I don't want you to push me into marrying you this way— especially when you can't even muster up enough manners to ask me properly!"

Luke shrugged. "If you want a proper proposal, we'd have to take the time to court, and I don't think I can spare that kind of time; I need help now and need to get married right away; that's why I went to the matchmaker— because I don't have time for romance. Marrying me would benefit you too; you'd have my help with the boy in your classroom, and you'd have more authority over him, but marrying me is the price to pay. Otherwise, you're on your own."

Lettie pursed her lips; he just didn't get it.

"Never mind; I'll handle it myself," she said.

Luke smirked. "Suit yourself, but I imagine you'll be begging my help inside of a few days."

"Don't be so prideful," she said.

Lettie walked away from Luke, feeling fiery anger rising from her gut; the man infuriated her almost to the point of exhaustion. She was not going to hang around him all day and put up with his coldness or his insults. If she couldn't talk Cassie into giving her a ride home, she would rather walk than to be near Luke another minute. And if he thought for a minute that she would agree to marry him now, he was in for a rude awakening if he dared to show up at the school to pick her up.

She walked down to the dock and sat on the end, kicking off her flip-flops and dangling her feet in the cold water. The leaves had already begun to turn, and several of them floated across the water in the breeze. Soon, the lake would be frozen over, and the community would be gathering for ice skating parties. She loved the season changes, but with that also brought another wedding season that would pass her by.

"Why so glum?"

Lettie turned around and shielded her eyes against the sun to peer into Cassie's green eyes that always held a bit of mischief in them.

"I just had an argument with Luke."

"What about?"

Lettie shrugged. "I'm not really sure—except that he won't propose to me."

Cassie giggled. "Is he supposed to be proposing to you?"

"We had supper together last night—which I'm sure you already know about since you talked me into taking food to him, but

Jordan Yoder showed up my *haus* just as I was leaving to take the food over there."

Cassie put her hand over her mouth to suppress a giggle.

"You sent him over there, didn't you?"

"I'm sorry," Cassie laughed. "I was talking to the matchmaker yesterday when he showed up, and I told her I finally talked you into taking food to him, but she told me she had just talked to your cousin, Annabelle, and told her to take food over the same night. So we figured we better send someone to let you both off the hook. She thought Annabelle might sway Luke into seeing you were the best choice—I mean—compared to Annabelle. She's too young and immature to be a *gut mudder* to the twins."

"The whole thing kind of blew up in my face," Lettie complained. "You two sabotaged our supper—in a way."

"Does that mean you had a nice supper together?" Cassie asked.

"*Nee!* The twins somehow railroaded us into getting married!"

100

"What? That's wonderful!" Cassie gushed.

"*Nee,* we came here together, but I want you to take me home; I don't want to be near him another minute. He only wants a marriage of convenience. You *know mei dat* will *never* allow me to marry for convenience; that, and I'm not twenty-five yet. You remember his dumb rule that his daughters can't marry until they've lived a little because he doesn't want us to regret staying in the community and being tied down to *kinner* at a young age, blah blah blah!"

"*Jah,* he is pretty strict, but my marriage started out between me and Ben for convenience, but we found love for each other, and now we are happy, and you can be with Luke," Cassie said. "That *mann* loves you—he always has. Tell your *vadder* that if he challenges you!"

"But Luke was always so irritating in school, and…"

"You were always *my* friend, and I was always getting into trouble in school, too," Cassie said, cutting her off. "But you know I

101

did it to get *mei vadder's* attention. I've told you a million times that Luke did all that stuff to get your attention."

"Causing me to break my arm certainly got my attention!" Lettie retorted.

Cassie let out a sigh as she lowered herself to the doc beside her friend. "Maybe it's time you forgave him for that; he was only twelve years old, and Lord only knows that twelve-year-old boys can't control themselves."

"He doesn't have that much control over himself as a grown *mann* either," Lettie complained.

Cassie smiled. "It's because of all that pent-up passion he has for you; you need to marry that *mann* so he'll calm down!"

Lettie's cheeks turned red hot.

"You love him; you always have," Cassie reminded her. "Don't let the past dictate your future with that *mann*. Do you want to see him marry someone else?"

Lettie lowered her head; she hadn't thought of that.

"Of course, I don't want him to marry someone else, but I'm not sure I'm ready to put away the past and marry a man who might remain a stranger to me for the rest of my life. Even if *mei dat* gives his permission, which we both know he won't, I've still got to get beyond the past. What if all we do is argue?"

"The only way to know is if you marry him quickly before your *dat* comes back!" Cassie advised. "Put out Luke's fiery passions and marry him!"

Was Cassie right Luke's fires of his passions put out by marrying him? The thought of being a wife to him put a fire in her that rose from her belly and settled on her cheeks.

CHAPTER EIGHT

Cassie pointed to Luke, who stood on the hill looking around. "Your betrothed is looking for you!"

"He's not my betrothed!" Lettie said, her heart pounding.

"He should be!" Cassie gushed. "He's so handsome; how could you say no to that *mann*—especially since you've been pining for him for so many years?"

"There's more to a marriage than physical attraction."

"Nee, but it helps!" Cassie said with a giggle. "And if you're going to get so hung up on formal proposals, you're never going to catch that *mann."*

"Ach, who says I want to catch him?" Lettie fumed.

"The dreamy look in your eyes and your pink cheeks every time I mention his name!"

Lettie groaned. "Just because we've been friends all our lives doesn't give you license to put words in my mouth."

"Nee, but I know your heart, Lettie, and I know how much you've pined for that *mann,"* Cassie said. "Stop being so prideful; if you have to watch him marry another woman, you'll be a miserable spinster, and I want you to be happy."

"How can I be happy with a *mann* who only wants me to keep his *haus* and be a *mudder* to the *kinner* he inherited?"

"My marriage started that way, but I found out it doesn't have to be that way at all," Cassie said. "Court him!"

"I have *three days* before the Bishop—your *vadder* is supposed to marry us, and I have to teach school; how can I court him in three days? Luke was right; he said the same thing. He doesn't have time to court me, and we don't have time for all the niceties of falling in love."

"The love is already there; I see the way he looks at you, and I know how you feel about him even if you're not willing to admit it. Let that love come out and get rid of the past; you have to forgive him for breaking your arm, or you will have a miserable marriage."

"If he loves me, why won't he tell me?" Lettie asked, anger souring her tone.

"*Menner* aren't as emotional as women, and they keep their feelings bottled up," Cassie said. "You're going to have to make the first move when it comes to talking about love, or you're never going to be able to marry that man—and tell him you forgive him already!"

"Who says I'm going to marry him?" Lettie said, crossing her arms in front of her.

"I don't think you could be that cruel and unforgiving toward Luke. Don't let him marry someone else out of a desperate need for a *mudder* for the twins; marry him and put both of you out of your misery."

"And what if we make each other miserable after we marry?" Lettie asked. "Then we'll be stuck."

"Marriage is work and love is a choice; you either choose to love him or you can choose to hold a grudge against him for the rest of your lives, in which case you'll be miserable."

Lettie puffed out her lower lip like a child. "I don't want to be miserable."

"Then leave the past where it belongs— in the past," Cassie advised her. "You're both grown up now; stop treating him like that boy who broke your arm so long ago. Luke needs a grown woman for his *fraa,* and the *kinner* need the same thing from you."

"Do you think he put the twins up to putting pressure on me to marry him and be their *mudder?* "

"Ach, I doubt it, but you'll never know for sure unless you ask him. From what you've been telling me for the last half hour, I'd have to say they have their own agenda. They overheard Luke talking to their *dat* and promising he'd marry you. So now they might think it's their job to get the two of you together since you're both so stubborn you can't do it on your own. Luke went along with it when they suggested it, didn't he? And wasn't he also the one to say it in the first place?"

Lettie nodded.

"So, that's your answer," Cassie said. "If he'd have objected when the *kinner* jumped on board, then you'd have a reason to be upset. Besides, he used you to get rid of Annabelle— a younger woman, which most *menner* would prefer so that right there should tell you he wants you to be his *fraa.*"

"Nee, it only shows he wants what is easy and comfortable."

Cassie chuckled. "You are anything but easy and comfortable; you're a difficult person to get along with, and I mean that with the utmost amount of love, but I know how stubborn you are because I've been your best friend ever since I can remember."

Lettie sighed. "Luke said I was difficult, but I think I just lack confidence."

Cassie hugged her. "Do you remember how bad I felt about my weight after having Simon, and you helped me get my confidence up so I could marry Ben? I think you're being just as tough on yourself as I was on myself about my big hips. It turns out; Ben loved me just the way I am. Trust me; Luke loves you just the way you are—he has since we were kids. Give him a break and court him—even if the only chance you get is the buggy ride home from the picnic with two *kinner* in the back of the buggy."

Lettie smirked. "How romantic!"

"It's not as bad as it sounds; my first date with Ben was with two *kinner* in the back of the buggy! It's what grownups do."

"I suppose you're right," Lettie relented.

"Of course I'm right," Cassie said with a smile. "Now go to your betrothed; he's looking for you!"

Lettie rose from the dock and brushed off the back of her dress, leaving her flip-flops where they were. "Do you really think I should marry him?"

"I think you'd be a fool not to," Cassie said.

They hugged, and Lettie slipped her feet into her flip-flops and walked up the dock to meet her betrothed. It was a foreign word to her and would take a bit of getting used to, but it was already growing on her.

****

Luke suppressed a smile when he saw Lettie walking toward him; he'd noticed her talking to Cassie and didn't want to interrupt. He hoped her friend was giving her some good advice, or at the very least, urging her to marry him. They'd been inseparable as children, and it had sometimes made it tough for him to get Lettie's attention away from Cassie; he supposed that was why he tried way too hard all the time, and it usually backfired on him, resulting in Lettie getting hurt somehow.

Lettie had brought up the incident where he'd caused her to fall and break her arm; did she still carry a grudge against him for that? He prayed not, but if she did, he would have to find a way to make that up to her. She'd mentioned she wanted him to court her, but Luke had no idea how that was going to work out since they only had three days before the wedding, and she had to teach school. He could invite her to take a buggy ride tomorrow evening, couldn't he? It didn't hurt to ask, he supposed. Now she headed in his direction, and he knew he needed to make up for the offensive comments he let escape his big mouth a little bit ago. It was time for him to stop hiding behind the twins like a coward and take control of his future—if he was to have one with Lettie.

She slowed her pace as she drew closer to him, taking the time to offer him a weak smile. He smiled back with a little more enthusiasm, hoping it would break the ice between them.

"The twins are asking if you'll eat with us," Luke said with downcast eyes. "I told them I'd ask you privately because I don't want you to feel pressured."

Lettie sighed, but then nodded with a weak smile. "*Jah,* I'd like to; *danki* for asking me."

Luke wondered why she might have added that last part except to send him an unspoken message that she liked being asked without having to tell him to ask her. He'd put her in a bad position to beg him for a proposal, and now he wished he could take it all back. If he'd acted like a man in the first place and proposed to her instead of using Annabelle to trick her into marrying him, they probably wouldn't be in this mess. Maybe his first mistake was in going to the matchmaker instead of going straight to Lettie and telling her how he felt about her.

****

Luke extended his arm to Lettie, and she tucked her hand in the crook of his elbow, the warmth of his skin sent prickles through her and stirred the butterflies in her stomach. She would have to stay as formal as possible with him, so she didn't lose her head; it wasn't practical or logical for her to get caught up with romantic thoughts of Luke if their marriage was to be for convenience reasons only. She prayed it wouldn't be, but until he gave her the right signal that it was anything but a practical wedding rather than wedded bliss, she would keep a cold wall around her heart.

When they reached the food table, all eyes turned to them, including the children, who rushed up to her and hugged her.

"I think we're going to have to start looking for a new schoolteacher!" the Bishop said with a chuckle.

Give up teaching school to marry Luke? She hadn't thought of that. She wanted to scream that she didn't want to give up teaching, but that was the way in their community. Only single women could teach, and she would have to choose between Luke and teaching. Couldn't she have both? Looking around at all the eyes on her and listening to each of the sudden bursts of *congratulations* from everyone, it dawned on Lettie that she was trapped, and there was no way she was getting out of marrying Luke—not that she wanted to.

Lettie hugged the twins as she admired the smile on Luke's face; it grew with every handshake from the men in the community. He soaked in every pat on the back, and all the woman rushed to her and took turns hugging her.

Whose fault was this mix-up? Luke's? The twins? Or what about the matchmaker and Cassie's interference? Maybe, just maybe, she was to blame for not speaking up, but she was too much in love with Luke to object to any of the shenanigans—except for the proposal—or lack thereof.

Lettie shrugged off the negativity and decided that since she couldn't fight it, she might as well try to embrace it. Within a few minutes, the women had promised her a dowry any bride would be jealous of and even offered to continue to bring supper over to them once they married so she would have time to adjust to being a mother and wife all at once. She thanked them with a genuine smile; they were all so kind and giving, it filled her with guilt for even thinking about rejecting the twins and their need for a mother. Being their mother was what God had in store for her future; the support of the community was confirmation enough for her.

CHAPTER NINE

Cassie was the last to hug Lettie while the other women went about dishing out food to their families. She pulled her close and whispered in her ear.

"Just breathe! Marrying Luke is what you've wanted for a long time, so don't fight it; go with it and enjoy your life. Make a future with Luke and love him so much he won't be able to help but love you back."

Lettie knew it was good advice, but it all happened so sudden that she was mixed up in her emotions, and they were hard for her to process. In less than twenty-four hours, she'd become engaged and was about to be a mother to two half-grown children. Three days from now, it would be final, and she'd no longer be the teacher. Was it wrong for her to mourn the loss of her identity as the teacher? Or would her new status as Luke's wife and the twins' mother be a good enough replacement to keep her happy? She loved teaching, but Cassie had given her something else to think about by reminding her that a mother was also a teacher.

As unsure as she was, she left her friend's side and stood beside Luke with her chin up and biting her lip so she wouldn't get upset. With every new step in life came changes, and it would be a significant change from being a teacher for the past five years to becoming a wife and instant mother overnight. Change was good; change meant progress, and being Luke's wife was indeed something she'd dreamed about many times. But never in her wildest dreams would she have thought she would marry him under these circumstances. Lettie was a grownup, and she had to put away her silly school-girl romantic notions of how her life would be with Luke. It would be whatever she made it; if she resisted and held back from Luke, it would likely be miserable, but if she forgave him and showered him with love no matter what he was doing, she'd be happy.

True happiness came from God—not from other people. It wasn't Luke's job to make her happy—it was hers and hers alone. Happiness, like love, was a choice, and she would have to choose to be content and to love him and the twins. She'd faced more significant challenges in her life than that. Besides, by making them happy, she'd make herself happy in the process; that was the way things worked.

****

Luke tried his best to go along with all the attention everyone was showering on him and Lettie about their wedding that he was still unsure about. For some reason, Lettie tried her best to resist him and had refused to agree to marry him unless he gave her a proper proposal, but yet here she was, soaking in all the attention right alongside him. Was it possible she was going to go through with the wedding on Wednesday, or would she make a fool of him and back out at the last minute? The same thing had happened to his cousin, Albert, and the poor guy had left and gone to another community to get away from all the ridicule. He couldn't pick up and leave the way Albert did because he had to think about the twins, who were deep-rooted in this community.

When the well-wishes began to die down, Luke welcomed Lettie at his side and offered his arm once more as they stood in line and waited for everyone to fill their plates. He loved these potluck dinners and looked forward to sampling a little of everything, Lettie's fried chicken, in particular.

"I hope there's still some of your fried chicken left by the time we make it through this line," he whispered to her.

"I sent the twins ahead of everyone to grab a couple of pieces for you," Lettie said, pointing to his niece and nephew, who were squeezing between folks to get their plates filled.

He smiled, thinking she'd just given him another reason to like her. Why hadn't he thought of that? Lettie was smart that way, but more than that, she'd thought about his needs without him having to say anything to her. Was it a sign that things might not be so bad for them as a married couple after all? He'd been so worried that things would be strained between them at best, but maybe it was time he started to trust her a little more and leave the worrying behind him.

"*Danki,*" he managed. "That was clever!"

She smiled, but it almost looked forced, and that bothered him; why was she holding back on him? One minute, she acted like she really cared about him, and the next, she acted reserved and nervous—almost as if she didn't trust him. Was she afraid he would break her heart this time instead of her arm? Broken bones healed fast, but a broken heart can sometimes stay with you a lifetime. He had to admit he had some fears that she would break his heart, but maybe it was time for him to give all of him to her and let her know her heart was safe with him—but how? Surely, a formal proposal wouldn't accomplish that. No, he had

120

to make some sort of grand gesture, didn't he? But what would be more dignified than a formal proposal? Flowers, maybe? No.

It wasn't until the twins came back with his fried chicken that he wondered if she wasn't using the kindness to heap burning coals on his head the way it says in the Bible. Did Lettie see the two of them as enemies? If that fried chicken were a heaping helping of burning coals, how was he going to get it down without it burning his stomach? He had to make peace with her—not to ease his own conscience, but it was the only way he was going to be able to live with her.

Luke took the fried chicken from the twins and forced a smile; he could already feel it souring in his gut. This was going to be a tough meal to swallow if every bite felt like burning coals going down his throat.

****

Lettie hadn't missed the distressed look on Luke's face when the twins rambled up to him with a plate of fried chicken for all of them to share. He'd almost sounded grateful when he'd thanked her, but when they'd presented it to him, he'd had a funny look on his face—as if it might come to life and bite off his nose with its beak. Did he not trust her? Surely, once he tried the chicken, he would like it. After all, it was the same way she always made it, and she'd noticed him going back for second helpings every time she brought it to the potluck dinners they had with the community. If she had to guess, it was one of his favorite dishes.

She'd always admired him from afar and had never acted on it. Had Cassie been right when she'd accused her of loving Luke all her life? Indeed, a woman doesn't pay that much attention to a man with whom she's not that interested.

They continued to go through the line, and Luke piled several things on the twins' plates, but she noticed he hadn't put anything on his plate yet. "Aren't you going to eat today?"

He tipped his head, not sure he understood what she meant until he saw his plate was empty. He cleared his throat. "I was so busy making sure the *kinner* got some food that I didn't even think about myself; I'll get some potatoes and biscuits to go with the fried chicken."

She smiled. She had in mind to get the same thing; maybe they had at least one thing in common—their taste for a good fried chicken meal. The only other thing they would have in common once they were married would be the twins, but she suspected the responsibility for them would fall mostly on her shoulders. He had a good trade as a farmer, and he would be a good provider, and she knew he worked hard for a man his age. Between that and helping his brother with his children, Luke had managed to put his personal life on hold for the sake of his family and didn't have time for romance. It was a commendable trait but a lonely one. It had been the same way with her teaching; she had devoted herself to the children in the community and had given up her chance to find romance for it. Was that something else they had in common?

The crisp autumn breeze made Lettie shiver, causing Luke to tuck his arm around her; he pushed the limits of public affection, but at the moment, she didn't care. She hadn't thought to bring her sweater from the buggy, but she was glad to see that the children had put on their light jackets. The warmth of Luke's arm around her sent shivers of a different kind down her spine; it was an odd but pleasant feeling she'd never experienced before. Was it love? There was no denying she loved the sense of security he was giving her, but it made her shake a little.

"Let me go to the buggy and get your sweater and a quilt so you'll be warm when we sit on the grass to eat," he said.

"*Danki,*" she said, taking his plate that he'd extended to her.

"Make sure to give me a heaping helping of mashed potatoes and gravy," he said with a smile.

They moved up in the line, and she filled the plates while Luke ran back to the buggy on the side yard of the Bishop's property where everyone had parked.

She shivered again without Luke's warmth around her anymore, but she hurried out of the shelter of the shade trees where they'd set up the food tables and into the sunshine where it was a little warmer. Last year, they'd had a scorching September and warm October, and so their autumn picnic had been a pleasant one. She suspected they would be seeing snow by the end of the month. It would make for a nice Thanksgiving, but she wasn't sure if she was ready for winter just yet, though she did love the season changes.

By the time Luke returned, the twins had found a beautiful spot in front of the lake to drop the quilt. Once he spread it out, Lettie put down the plates of food, and Luke startled her when he draped her sweater over her shoulders. His touch sent shivers through her again, and she turned toward the sun to avoid having her heated cheeks seen by him. When they were all settled, Luke reached out a hand to her and Ellie, who took Eli's hand for the silent prayer. Lettie found it challenging to concentrate on the quiet time but managed to ask God for confirmation that she was making the right choice by being here with Luke and the children. She also asked to put love in their hearts if they were to be married because she didn't want to suffer through a loveless marriage.

All too soon, she felt Luke's hand slip away from hers, and she opened her eyes and lifted her head in time to see the children already digging into their plates. Luke did the same, and they sat in silence most of the remainder of the meal, except for Eli pointing out several times how he was going to finish eating first and race his sister to the dessert table. She started to argue with him at first but then slowed down when he gloated over being way ahead of her in the *eating race.*

"Slow down," Luke warned him. "This food is too *gut* to gobble; take the time to appreciate the chicken that Miss Fisher made for us."

"When can we call her *Mamm?*" Eli whined.

"I'll let you know," Luke reprimanded them. "Eat!"

He'd put off answering their question for now, but Lettie could see in their eyes that they were not going to let it go that easily.

CHAPTER TEN

Cassie helped Lettie set up the dessert table by unwrapping all the sugary treats while the other women packed away the leftover food from the meal.

"How can I get Luke to talk to me?" Lettie complained. "Aside from getting me my sweater and putting his arm around me, he barely paid any attention to me all afternoon—except to thank me for getting the twins to sneak ahead of the line to get him some fried chicken. I don't want to marry a *mann* who isn't capable of carrying on a conversation with me—or who might not even want to talk to me. Who wants to live in silence with a spouse their entire life?"

"If you don't want to marry Luke, then I will, Cousin!" Annabelle said, coming up from behind them. "I wouldn't care if he ever said a word to me; I'd be too busy kissing him anyway!"

Cassie shooed the girl with her hand. "You shouldn't be eavesdropping on other people's conversations! Go find a *mann* your own age because Lettie is marrying Luke."

Annabelle smirked. "Doesn't sound like it to me! As for Luke, we'll just see which one of us he wants more."

Cassie laughed at her. "Didn't he send you home last night when you brought supper to him?"

Annabelle fumed. "He did not; I left voluntarily when the spinster showed up and interrupted our meal. I lost my appetite; that's all."

"*Ach,* don't call me a spinster," Lettie barked at her. "If you want to get technical, you're a spinster too!"

"*Jah,* but the difference between us, Cousin, is that you're too old to get married,"

"I'm not too old for Luke to propose to!" Lettie shot back.

"I don't believe Luke proposed yet, and that's why you're riding the fence," Annabelle said, glaring at her. "But it doesn't matter because now you've got some competition."

"Go ahead and do whatever you think you have to, Annabelle," Cassie warned the teenager. "But *mei vadder* is marrying Lettie and Luke on Wednesday, and you won't be there—not as a guest, and certainly not as the bride!"

She guffawed. "We'll just see about that!" Annabelle turned on her heels and walked away from them and sat next to Luke, flashing them a satisfied smile.

Lettie groaned. "What if Luke changes his mind about marrying me and decides he'd rather marry Annabelle instead?" Lettie asked, worry bubbling up from her gut.

Cassie giggled. "He won't, but at least now you know how you really feel about Luke."

"What are you talking about?"

Cassie rolled her eyes. "All it took was a couple of misplaced words from your very competitive cousin, and you get a bad case of the green-eyed monster trying to claw its way out of your heart!"

"*Ach,* I'm not jealous of Annabelle!"

"Maybe you're not jealous of her personally, but you are jealous that she's sitting next to your betrothed, trying desperately to get his attention."

Lettie chuckled. "A lot of good it's doing her," she said, gesturing toward Luke. "Look at him; he's ignoring her."

Cassie sucked in her breath. "As long as you don't think he's ignoring her only because you're over here watching him!"

Lettie groaned. "Now, you're trying to stir the pot, Cassie."

She smirked. "Is it working?"

"If you mean, am I going to go over there and make a fool of myself by throwing myself at Luke to get Annabelle to leave, then no," Lettie said. "I'm going to walk away and trust him to decide on his own without me breathing down the back of his neck."

Cassie smiled. "I'm proud of you; you're showing Annabelle that you're not threatened by her competitive and immature tricks, and I'm happy to see that you trust Luke."

She sighed. "If only I could trust him with my heart."

Cassie looped her arm in hers, and they walked back toward Ben, who sat in the shade with their two sleeping babies.

"Pray about it," Cassie urged her. "Only *Gott* can give you the answer you're looking for." She pointed behind Lettie's head. "Don't look now, but your betrothed managed to shake his immature shadow, and he's coming this way."

Lettie felt her heart pounding wildly.

"The twins want to go stick their feet in the lake," Luke said, causing her to turn around and face him. "They wanted you to come along if you're not busy."

Ben rose from the quilt, and the two men shook hands; it did her heart good to see them get along because they'd never been close, and it was important to her that she be able to keep a close friendship with Cassie if she married Luke. Having her friend's husband be able to hang out with her husband while they engaged in *girl-talk* was vital.

Within a few minutes, they were bidding the couple goodbye, and Luke whisked her off to the lake, where the twins were waiting for them so they could sink their feet in the water. Though Lettie had put her feet in earlier, she'd gotten a chill from it and was a little unsure if the children should put their feet in the cold lake water or not, but she wasn't going to undermine Luke's authority over them.

"You might want to leave your coats on," she advised the twins. "The water is a little chilly this time of the year."

"Okay, *Mamm,*" Eli said with a mischievous smile.

She smiled back, butterflies stirring in her gut as she waited for Luke to correct the child, but the man kept quiet. It wasn't her place to correct Eli, especially since she admittedly liked the sound of being called *mamm*—even if she wasn't his mother—yet.

****

Luke assisted Lettie into the buggy; it had been a long afternoon, and the twins had not tired of splashing around in the water until they'd nearly soaked each other to the skin. Luke wrapped both lap blankets around them to keep them warm on the way home, which left Lettie without a lap quilt, and she was a little chilly. She scooted over in her seat while Luke went around to the other side of the buggy to get in, hoping he wouldn't notice she'd moved closer. She told herself she'd only done it to get warm, but she had in mind to be nearer him on the long drive home. He climbed in and moved as close as possible to her, tucking an arm around her, which brought immediate heat to her cheeks.

"I wouldn't want you to be too cold," he said. "I didn't bring a coat today, or else I would have put that around you."

"This is better," she said barely above the buggy noise.

He chuckled and pulled her a little closer. Lettie wasn't about to complain; she was perfectly content to be in his arms. Had she finally let go of the animosity between them? All she knew was that she wasn't feeling anything but love for him right now, and that was a good thing. If she could completely move past it and let her guard down, they would likely have an easier time of their impending marriage that appeared to be orchestrated by two very clever children.

They'd been quiet for the last mile or so, and Lettie looked over her shoulder to check on the twin in the back seat. "They're sleeping!" she said with a giggle.

"They've had a long day," Luke said, steering the horse onto the county road that led to her farm.

They'd all had a long day; Lettie's emotions had gone from one extreme to the other all day, and it had worn her out. Right now, as she sat dangerously close to Luke, her emotions were the strongest they'd been. Her head was swimming, and she was helpless against his forwardness, but having his arm around her made her feel giddy. Would this feeling last, or would her bliss escape her as soon as he dropped her off? All she knew was that she wasn't acting like herself; she wasn't even feeling much like herself, and she wasn't sure what was happening between them, but something was.

****

Luke turned the corner onto Lettie's street; how had they gotten this far so soon? He'd spent the entire ride trying to decide if he was going to kiss her goodnight or not, but now that they were so close, he was losing his nerve. It wasn't that he didn't want to kiss her, but he feared rejection if he should try. They had a stormy history, and he wasn't about to risk losing his only chance with her when she was so close to becoming his wife. He assured himself there would be plenty of time for kissing once they were married; surely, he could control his urges for two more days, couldn't he? The truth was, he didn't want to; he wanted more than anything to pull her close and claim her lips and all the rest of her too.

"Stop!" Lettie said.

Luke jumped, his dreamy gaze sharpening. *Was I thinking out loud?*

"You missed the turn," Lettie said.

Sure enough, he'd somehow managed to drive right past her driveway. "I'm sorry; I can turn around," he said. "I guess I was on autopilot and headed toward my place."

In a few days, if Lettie agreed to marry him, it would be her place, too, but it wasn't yet no matter how much his subconscious might want it to be. The corners of his mouth lifted into a dreamy smile.

"What are you smiling about?" she asked.

"Nothing really," he fibbed.

"Now, you *must* tell me!"

He smirked. "If you really need to know what I was thinking, I thought it would be nice to take you home with me."

Lettie sat upright with a gasp and scooted over to the far edge of the buggy seat.

"Well—if that isn't the most improper proposal I've ever heard!"

Luke slapped a hand against his forehead and shook his head. "*Ach,* I didn't mean it like that!"

She furrowed her brow. "Then what did you mean?"

He shrugged. "I only meant that it would be nice just to go home once we're married—without me having to drop you off."

Lettie's frame went rigid in her seat, and she raised her chin slightly. "I still haven't agreed to marry you."

Luke sighed. "I thought we had this settled; don't tell me you're still holding out for a proposal."

Lettie turned her head away from him. "What if I am?"

"Then, you'll be waiting for the rest of your life because I'm not a romantic sort of *mann,* and I'm not going to be coerced into proposing."

Lettie sucked in her breath. "And I'm not going to be coerced into marrying you while you hide behind the *kinner.*"

Luke pulled his buggy into her driveway and stopped near the back porch. He hopped down to assist her out, but she was already halfway to her kitchen door.

"Lettie, wait!" he called out to her. "Can't we talk about this?"

Lettie turned on her heels. "What is there to talk about?"

"We had such a *gut* day, and I don't want to part ways like this; the Bible says we shouldn't let the sun go down on our anger, and it's nearly dark. Can't we mend fences?"

Lettie drew in a breath; he was right, and he was calling her out. Did she dare back down and let him off the hook, or would she regret it? She decided to stand her ground even though she didn't have much of a leg to stand on. Here this man was offering her marriage and a life that didn't involve spending her days—and nights as a lonely spinster, and she was pushing her luck with him by being so demanding and rigid.

"If you have something to say to me—or to *ask* me—I'm listening."

"Lettie Fisher, you're impossible," he barked.

"And you have no manners!" she shot back.

Luke planted his fists on his hips and scowled. "You're infuriating!"

"And you're…"

Luke closed the space between them and pressed his lips to hers, and she suddenly forgot everything she had in mind to say to him.

CHAPTER ELEVEN

Luke swept his lips across Lettie's, unable to think about anything except deepening the kiss and taking things to a marital level, but he was determined to keep it respectful. His impulsive behavior managed to shut her up, but the way she responded sent shivers of desire to make her his bride surge through him like static electricity.

Lettie raked her fingers through his thick hair, sending shivers down the back of his neck.

"Say you'll marry me," he begged her in between kisses.

Was that his voice asking? He was so far lost in her kisses; he must have lost his head, but he wouldn't take it back; he meant it. He hadn't planned to give in to her this way, but he couldn't help himself; he was in love with her, and if a proposal was what she wanted, he'd just given it to her.

"*Jah,*" she whispered. "I'll marry you."

Luke pulled away from her long enough to look into her dreamy eyes and flash her a smile. His kisses made her giggle, but those kisses were sincere.

"*Onkel* Luke!" Ellie called from the buggy.

Luke broke away from Lettie and cleared his throat. "I don't think they should see us like this. Can I take you for a buggy ride tomorrow?"

He squeezed her hands and smiled.

Her eyes lit up, and she returned his smile. "*Jah,* I'd love to."

He leaned in and pecked her on the cheek. "I'll pick you up at seven o'clock."

He turned to leave, and she called out to him. "Wait; I have to tell you something."

Luke waved over his shoulder. "It'll have to wait until tomorrow; I gotta take them home!" He ran back toward the buggy just in time to keep Ellie from climbing out and coming after him.

"I'm tired; I wanna go home," she whined.

"Let's go home and get you tucked into your warm bed," he said, pulling the lap quilt back over her.

She yawned and closed her eyes, and Luke slapped the reins against his gelding's flank and headed toward their farm. If he was going to be bringing a bride home with him in a couple of days, he had a lot of work to get done to make the house welcoming to her.

****

Lettie bolted upright in her bed when the rooster crowed; she'd barely slept all night from thinking about Luke and her upcoming wedding, but she'd just dozed off, and that pesky rooster had interrupted a good dream.

In the kitchen, she put on a pot of coffee and replayed last night's scene on her back porch as she drew her hands to her lips that still tingled from Luke's kiss.

She let loose a giddy squeal. "I'm getting married," she gushed.

She was getting married to the only man she'd ever loved, and she had so much to do. Grateful today was not a church Sunday; she made a mental note of everything she wanted to get done before Luke arrived to take her for her first buggy ride ever. Was it strange that she'd already experienced her first kiss and gotten the proposal she wanted *before* the buggy ride? She giggled; that was what her father would have called *putting the cart before the horse,* but in her case, it was placing the kiss and the proposal before the courting. Now her only worry was rushing through the next couple of days until the wedding before her parents decided to come home.

Lettie couldn't wait to tell Cassie every detail about last night. Her friend had told her she was coming over today to help her pack her things; had Cassie somehow known all along Luke was going to propose? It didn't matter; all that mattered was that she got the proposal. She would welcome Cassie's help and support though she hated marrying Luke without her family there. If not for the fact that she had to marry him behind her father's back, she wouldn't be getting married at all—at least not until her twenty-fifth birthday, and that was more than three months away. Luke had warned her he had no time to lose, and she was glad of that because she didn't either. She suspected he wanted to marry this wedding season and before winter set in so they would be settled, and she understood that, but her father was an unbending man and would object just to make sure she followed his rules. It had surprised her that they'd left her alone in the house for so many months, but she supposed they didn't see her as being as rebellious as Annie was. Her sister had always been boy-crazy and had potential beaus showing up at the house consistently. Lettie had not had one caller; it was one of the reasons she'd agreed to take the teaching position when the Bishop offered it just after her eighteenth birthday when the previous teacher left to marry that wedding season. Her first year had been a difficult one because she was only a couple of years older than her eighth-grade students, but the following year, she was more established, and the students began to take her more seriously as the years wore on.

Now, as she gazed out the window at the colorful leaves blowing about the yard in the sharp autumn wind, she wondered if she should tell Luke about her father's objections. He'd not said one word about her family attending the wedding; all he'd said was that they would go before the Bishop after hours and no one in the community would be there to help them celebrate their marriage of *convenience*. Would the Bishop still consider it a marriage in name only since they'd kissed? Maybe that was a question Cassie could answer for her. If it were anything besides a marriage of convenience, she would think they would have to wait until wedding season, and the entire community—including her parents, would be there to witness the marriage. She didn't want to wait that long; it gave too many weeks for her father to find reasons to object, including the fact that she wouldn't turn twenty-five until after the wedding season ended.

Luke would not wait that long for her; she was sure of that.

Lettie shivered when the wind whistled through the windowpane, making her wish Luke was there with her to hold her in his warm embrace. The first week of October had brought a cold wind nearly every day, and her mind was already filling with visions of long winter nights in front of a warm fireplace snuggled up with Luke. She wrapped her arms around her middle and hugged herself against the chill in the kitchen. With her parents away, she might consider wearing a pair of leggings with a sweatshirt today while she packed instead of her usual work dress. Cassie wouldn't say anything, and she wouldn't be going out anywhere until later when Luke showed up for their buggy ride. Her smile widened as she turned off the burner and poured herself a cup of coffee, as she imagined pouring a second cup for her husband to tie him over until she made his breakfast.

Lettie sighed and tipped her head to look out into the blustery day; would her life with Luke be as romantic as she hoped it would be? Cassie had told her she could make it as romantic as she wanted; all she had to do was be a good wife and keep his belly full of hot food. She giggled at the thought of making a man happy just by feeding him plenty of good food and keeping his house neat and tidy. She did that here at home for her parents, but the difference would be she'd get to kiss Luke every day—that was something a woman only got if she was married. Cassie had warned her that marriage was a lot of hard work, too, but the benefits were worth it. She couldn't wait to spend every day and every night with Luke.

****

By the time Cassie showed up at her farm, Lettie was halfway through her list of things to get done before she began the actual packing process. Most important to her had been to thoroughly clean the room so her mother wouldn't be burdened with the task after she'd moved out. She'd spent hours scrubbing the floors and dusting the room from top to bottom and polished the wood furniture. She'd washed the quilts and put them away in the closet. She would use the wool blanket for the next couple of nights if she got cold, even though she wasn't fond of the itchy material. The truth was, she wouldn't have time to clean the room or the linens before her wedding Wednesday afternoon. She would dress the bed in the quilts when she left for school on the day of the wedding so she wouldn't forget.

A light knock followed by a call of *hello* brought Lettie to the top of the stairs.

"Up here, Cassie," she hollered down.

Lettie went back to her room and started folding her clothes and laying them out on the bed. "I've just started packing; I wanted to get the room cleaned first," she said when Cassie entered the room.

Cassie handed her a package wrapped in plain brown paper.

Lettie smiled as she took the gift. "What's this?"

"Just open it," Cassie said with a giggle.

Lettie's heart pounded as she hesitated, wondering if it was something intimate for her wedding night with Luke. She felt her cheeks warm as she let out a little giggle.

She turned the package over and untied the twine that bound it, and lifted a blue dress from the folds of brown paper. She sucked in her breath and looked at Cassie with wide eyes.

"When did you have time to make this?"

"I started it a few days ago," Cassie said. "I didn't want you to marry Luke without a proper dress."

"Danki, it's perfect!" Lettie pulled her friend into a hug, tears welling up in her eyes.

She held the dress up to her, noting the delicate stitching on the white organdy apron that tied around the back of the dress.

"I tied the prayer *kapp* to the back," Cassie said, showing her.

Lettie untied it from the apron strings and removed the one on her head, replacing it with the delicate organdy *kapp* used for weddings. "I'm going to look like a real bride," she gushed. "Even if no one will be at the ceremony."

"Your husband will see you in the dress, and he's the only one who counts," Cassie said with a giggle.

Lettie's face tingled with fresh heat when she let out a giggle. "I hope he doesn't think I had it waiting around for the past ten years waiting for a proposal."

"You can tell him I made it for you," Cassie said. "We wouldn't want him to think you've been waiting around for him all this time; it might puff up his ego too much."

Lettie giggled. "Even though it is the truth!"

"It might make him appreciate you more if he knew how long you've waited for him, but I have a feeling he's been waiting for you just as long."

Lettie nodded and smiled. "*Jah,* you're probably right about that, but we can both keep that to ourselves."

Cassie pulled her into another hug. "The important thing is that you're finally getting to be with the *mann* you love."

"Not if I don't get this stuff packed and waiting by the back door," Lettie said. "Luke wants to pick it up Wednesday when he picks me up to take me to school. I have to leave *dat's* buggy and horse here. Luke said he could come over and feed the animals until my parents get back from Annie's *haus.*"

"Why can't you do it?"

Lettie shrugged. "I guess I could go after school."

Cassie's face soured.

"What's wrong?"

"Didn't *mei dat* tell you?"

Lettie shook her head. "Tell me what?"

"He has a replacement teacher," Cassie said. "She's supposed to start on Thursday."

Lettie's heart pounded, and her breath hitched.

"I'm sorry; I thought you knew."

Lettie collapsed onto the edge of the bed; she hadn't been prepared to give up teaching so soon, but she knew the rules. She wasn't allowed to teach school once she married, but she hadn't expected it to hit her so hard.

"I'm fine," she said, hoping to convince herself.

Would marrying Luke fill the gap of teaching? It was all she'd known since her eighteenth birthday. Change was good, and she was excited to be marrying the man she loved, but how long would she mourn the loss of losing her job as a teacher?

****

Luke dropped off the twins at his neighbor's house after they volunteered to watch them while he took Lettie for a buggy ride. Things were moving fast between them, but he didn't mind; his head was spinning a little out of control, but he was in love and couldn't be happier.

When he pulled his horse into her driveway, he couldn't wipe the silly grin from his face even if he tried. After he tied up his horse, he skipped toward the back door and knocked. He was so excited to see her, and it was tough for him to contain his emotions.

Lettie opened the door and failed to greet him with her usual smile; her eyes were pink-rimmed, and her face looked puffy as if she'd been crying. He closed the space between them and kissed her lightly on the cheek.

"What's wrong?" he asked, his tone gentle and quiet. "Did something happen?"

Lettie raised her chin. "I'm a little tired and got too much dust in my eyes while I was cleaning today," she said.

Luke knew her better than that. Her elevated chin told him she was not happy with him for some reason. What could he have done wrong between last night's kisses and today's buggy ride? He hadn't been anywhere near her.

"This is not the way to start a marriage," he said. "I can see that you've been crying, and I can't help but feel it has something to do with me."

"Only indirectly," she said sniffling. "But it isn't something you did."

Luke blew out a breath. "I'm sure it is, and I didn't do it intentionally, whatever it is."

"Nee, I'll get over it, but it might take some time."

Luke closed the space between them and put a finger under her chin to make her look at him. "Whatever it is, I'm sure I owe you an apology."

Lettie started to shake her head, but he gave her a stern look.

"Don't discount this; I've owed you an apology for a lot of years," he said. "When you broke your arm that day, I was only trying to make you laugh because I liked you; I know that's not a good excuse, and I'm not trying to make one, but I was just a dumb boy, and I had no idea you were going to get frightened and trip over the woodpile. I didn't do it to break your arm; I loved your laugh and wanted to be the one to make you laugh, but it turns out, I made you cry, and I've felt like a heel ever since that day."

Her eyes softened, and the corners of her mouth lifted into a smile. "I had no idea you were trying to make me laugh; I thought you were being mean."

Luke's throat clogged with a lump. "I could never be mean to you—even though now that I'm an adult, I can see how you might have taken it that way. I had such a big crush on you, and all I wanted to do was to make you happy."

Her smile grew, and it warmed his heart. "You do make me happy, but I have some apologizing of my own to do."

His eyes bulged, and he chuckled. "You? What do you have to apologize to me for?"

"For holding a grudge against you for so many years," she answered. "I should have forgiven you right away."

"How could you have forgiven me when I've taken all this time to say I was sorry to you?"

Lettie giggled. "You don't need an apology from someone to forgive them—

although it is helpful—and nice to hear finally."

"I feel a lot better knowing you finally forgive me," Luke said with a chuckle.

"I have something else to say to you," Lettie said, her expression turning serious.

Luke felt his heart skip a beat; was she about to turn the tables on him and take back her acceptance to his proposal?

"You said something the other day about you not being the ideal *mann* in my eyes," she began. "I need you to know that isn't true; you're everything I could ever want in a *mann*. I've loved you my whole life. It started as a crush when we were in school, but as the years wore on, I went from admiring you from afar to full-out falling in love with you. It might have been one-sided in my mind, but now I know that my love for you was not in vain. I'm proud of the *mann* you've turned out to be— for the way you stepped in and gave up your own life to help your *brudder,* and for the way you stepped into his shoes as a *vadder* to the twins when he passed away. I'd be proud to call you my husband," Lettie admitted.

"I'm glad you feel that way about me; it makes me feel better about the past," he said. "Maybe now we can put all of that behind us and leave it in the past where it belongs."

"I agree," she said.

"Now, are you going to tell me why you were so upset when I got here?" he asked. "I really want to know."

She lowered her gaze. "Cassie told me the Bishop already found a replacement teacher for my classroom; she's due to take over on Thursday."

"I'm sorry, Lettie," he said. "I know how much teaching means to you."

"It's going to seem strange sending the twins off to school to be taught by another teacher," Lettie said. "I'm not going to know what to do with myself all day during school hours."

Luke waggled his eyebrows. "I'm hoping you'll want to spend a lot of that time with me—in private—getting to know me better!"

Lettie's cheeks turned red, and he found it so adorable, he couldn't stop himself from pressing his lips to hers.

CHAPTER TWELVE

Lettie's shoulders arched from their drooped position when Luke mentioned them spending time alone as husband and wife. His warm lips on hers sent tingles through her like twinkly lights at Christmas time. He wrapped his arms around her and used them to draw her closer to his solid frame, sending sparks of excitement all the way to her toes. Spending time alone with Luke was dangerous the way she felt right now; she didn't trust herself not to lose herself in his kisses.

Lettie pulled away from him slightly and let out a giggle. "Weren't we going to take a buggy ride?"

Luke separated from her and cleared his throat. "*Jah,* we probably should go before we get too carried away," he said with a chuckle.

****

Luke steered the buggy into the grassy area on the other side of the lake; being a Sunday night, he expected more of the youth to be gathered here by now, but he supposed the Sunday night singing hadn't let out yet. Once again, they were secluded, and he wasn't sure if he trusted himself to be alone with her for too long. Perhaps if they got out and walked down to the dock, it would give him a little more control over his urges to kiss her under the moonlight.

Hopping down from the buggy, he lifted Lettie's wispy frame down and made it a point to take her hand. He led her toward the dock while he pointed out the constellations. Though he would rather gaze into her dreamy brown eyes, it was important to him that he built trust with her to safeguard her virtue. They strolled down to the end of the dock, the wind coming off the lake was chilly, the water a bit choppy. It was probably why they were the only couple here tonight.

Lettie pulled her cape around her, and Luke tucked his arm around her. The wind howled; it was too cold for the usual bullfrogs to surface and sing them a song, and the night lacked summer sounds. Winter was settling in, and he was eager to be married and settled before the first snow. Admittedly, he looked forward to Thanksgiving and Christmas with Lettie, hoping that the twins' first holiday without their father would somehow be better with a woman in the house as their new mother.

"What are you thinking about so intensely?"

Lettie's question took him by surprise.

"Thanksgiving—and those turkeys that Eli chased home," he said with a chuckle. "You know I'm going to have a tough time convincing him to eat one of them. He named them!"

"I'm almost afraid to ask what he named them," she said with a giggle.

"Bishop Gobbler and *Frau* Gobbler!"

Lettie threw her head back and laughed. "Why would he name them that?"

"Because he insists that they look like the Bishop and his *fraa*," Luke said, unable to contain his laughter. "He wants me to make a small Bishop hat to put on his head."

"I'm not sure you should tell the Bishop, but I'm going to have to tell Cassie; she'll get a kick out of it."

"I'm afraid I'm going to have to find another turkey somewhere, or we'll be having roast chicken for Thanksgiving this year," Luke complained.

"He was chasing four of them that day; I'm surprised he managed to get two of them home!"

Luke chuckled. "Me too! If there's more in the area, I can probably bag one for the meal, but I'll have to keep him somewhere safe so that Eli doesn't try to give him a name or we'll be back to eating chicken."

"I'm sure we can keep them in the henhouse at my farm—*mei dat's* farm," Lettie said with a giggle at her correction. "In a few days, it will simply be my childhood home."

"Are you okay with marrying me without your *familye* here?"

She nodded. "*Jah, mei vadder* forbid me to marry until I'm twenty-five."

Luke blew out a breath. "Why would he do that?"

"Because he wants to be sure I experience things other than being a farmer's *fraa*. He thinks because he and *mei mudder* got married so late in life that most of the youth who marry in the community so young aren't mature enough to make that decision."

"I just turned twenty-five, so your birthday couldn't be too far away."

Lettie sighed. "I'm afraid so; it's after the wedding season. So he would insist we have a long engagement and wait until next season."

"I would have preferred to get your *vadder's* permission to marry you," Luke said. "But as long as you're okay with marrying me without that, I'd prefer not to wait. "I guess I was so caught up in everything I hadn't really given it much thought until now."

"I don't want to wait either," Lettie gushed.

"Then we won't," Luke assured her. "The Bishop suggested we get married quietly anyway because of the circumstances."

Lettie raised an eyebrow at his statement. "What *circumstances?"*

"Ach, you know; us getting married for convenience reasons—to give *mei brudder's kinner* two parents."

Luke felt Lettie's frame turn rigid under his arm.

"Did I say something wrong?"

She shook her head, but he knew better; he knew her body language, and even if he had to pull it out of her, she was going to talk about her feelings with him. They were, after all, about to be married, and communication was important between two people who loved each other.

That's it; she doesn't think I love her!

"You do *know* that our marriage is no longer a marriage of convenience—at least it isn't for me," he said.

"It's not?" she asked. "If not, then the Bishop will probably make us wait until wedding season a few weeks from now to be married."

Luke shrugged. "We don't have to tell him things have changed between us, but we'll know."

Lettie was quiet.

"I love you," he said, turning around and pulling her into his arms. "I don't want to wait to marry you; I can barely wait three days!"

Lettie giggled. "I love you too, Luke, and I can't wait to marry you either."

Luke pulled her close and smiled. "Maybe we don't have to!"

Lettie's eyes grew wide. "What do you mean? Who is going to marry us at eight o'clock at night?"

"The Bishop doesn't go to bed until nine o'clock," he said. "I know this because I always make his delivery last when I do a haymow, and then I stay for tea and cookies afterward. It's the last farm on my route and closest to home."

Lettie nodded. *"Jah,* when we were young, and I would stay overnight with Cassie, I remember them going to bed an hour later than my parents—because he's not a farmer."

"We can walk up the hill and see if he's willing; all he can do is say no."

Lettie giggled and lowered her head. "What reason will you give him for the rush? Won't he be suspicious if we show up out of the blue?"

"Nee, he asked if I wanted him to perform the ceremony this evening after

167

supper, but I told him I might need more time to convince you," Luke said.

"I didn't need convincing to be in love with you," she said. "Because I've loved you on some level most of my life."

"I've probably loved you longer," he said with a chuckle. "But you weren't exactly on board with marrying me."

"I think I was in my heart, but my brain was somehow blocking me," she admitted. "If that makes any sense."

"I think I understand what you mean." He said, taking her hand and leading her up the hill to the Bishop's house. "But it doesn't matter anymore because in a few minutes, if the Bishop is willing, we'll be married."

Her hand tightened on Luke's, bringing him to a halt. "What is it?"

"I don't have the dress that Cassie made me for the wedding," she said, biting her bottom lip.

"Is it that important?" he asked.

"I promised her I'd wear it since she practically stayed up night and day all week to make it for me."

"If we go back to get it, we won't have time to get married," Luke warned her. "The Bishop will go to bed, and we'll lose our window."

"Then I'll wear it to church on Sunday when we attend together for the first time!" she said with a giggle.

Luke leaned in and kissed her on the mouth and then hurried her up the rest of the hill toward the Bishop's house. When they reached the back door, Lettie pulled on his hand again.

"What if he says no?"

Luke shrugged. "Then I suppose we'll have to wait until Wednesday."

She nodded, and Luke knocked on the door.

The Bishop answered the door moments later, a knowing smile on his face. "I had a feeling I'd be getting a visit from the two of you when I heard your buggy pull in down by the lake."

"I hope we didn't disturb you," Luke offered.

He chuckled. "*Nee,* I bought the property surrounding the lake so that I could keep a watchful eye on the youth. I was expecting you to show up tonight; I'm guessing you're ready to be married now?"

Luke nodded. "*Jah,*"

Lettie smiled and nodded, casting her eyes downward.

"Come in and let's get started so I can get to sleep on time," he said with a smile.

He welcomed them into the sitting room and helped them get comfortable while he fetched his book to perform the nuptials. "If you don't mind, we'll skip the sermon and get right to the ceremony," he said. "I don't think we need to have a drawn-out service this late at night."

Both Lettie and Luke nodded in agreement. Luke was eager to get his bride home and settled in, and since they would still have to go back to her house to get her things, it was going to be a long night. It was a good thing the Bielers had agreed to keep the twins overnight and take them to school in the morning with their children, who were the same age. Luke was happy he'd had the forethought to ask them to keep the twins overnight, thinking that he'd have a late night with their buggy ride. At least this way, they would have some privacy on their wedding night. He pushed away the thoughts that brought heat to his face when the Bishop called them to stand before him so he could marry them.

****

Lettie leaned her head on Luke's shoulder the entire ride back to her house; she was in a dreamy state—especially after Luke had pulled off to the side of the deserted country road to shower her with kisses they could not share after the ceremony. That was not allowed until they were in private, but she was happy he'd stopped, declaring he couldn't wait another minute to kiss her. She hadn't been able to wait either, but they didn't waste any time getting back on the road. Bishop Troyer had granted her permission to continue teaching for at least tomorrow so he could make arrangements with the new teacher to take over a couple of days early, so she would have to get up early to make it to school. She knew there would be some adjustments to be made once they got her cedar trunk back to his house, and then she had to assume they would consummate the marriage before going to sleep. It was exciting that they had such an evening ahead of them before they could retire for the night; she was too giddy to be sleepy anyway.

When they pulled into her driveway, something was amiss. She hadn't remembered leaving the kitchen light on when she'd left. It hadn't been dark when Luke had picked her up; had she turned it on thinking ahead that it would be practical to have it on when she returned?

She sat up and looked at the house, the hair on the back of her neck prickling.

"What's wrong?" Luke asked after he stopped the buggy.

"I'm not sure," she said, staring at the kitchen window, her heart pounding in her ears.

"Did you leave that light on in the kitchen?"

She shrugged. "I don't remember."

"Do you want me to go inside and check the *haus* first?"

She shook her head. "*Nee,* I don't think I want to be left out here alone."

"Well, then let's go see if everything is alright," he said, hopping down and taking her hand. "I'm sure you left the light on so you wouldn't have to come home to a dark *haus.*"

"*Jah,* I think you're right," she said, trying to convince her heart rate to slow down.

When they entered the kitchen, she noticed her trunk wasn't by the door where she'd left it; she and Cassie had carried it down the stairs before filling it, and now it was no longer there. She pointed to the empty spot. "My trunk is gone!"

A noise from the hallway startled her, and she backed up toward the door behind Luke; it came from the direction of her parents' room.

"Lettie; is that you?" her mother called out.

Lettie put a hand to her chest and let out the breath she'd been holding in with a whoosh.

"*Jah, Mamm,* it's me!"

Her mother entered the kitchen, and Lettie went to her and hugged her. "I've missed you, but why didn't you send word you were coming home today? You nearly took ten years off my life when I heard a noise and saw the lights on; I didn't know if we might be walking in on a break-in!"

"What are you doing out so late?" her father barked from the hallway.

Lettie gulped. "*Dat,* I'm sorry; I didn't mean to wake you."

"Did you think I was going to go to sleep before you got home?" he barked. "Where have you been this late at night with Lucas King? Your horse and buggy are still in the barn, so I know you didn't have trouble on the road. And what was the meaning of you packing your trunk? You were going to marry without your *familye* here with you?"

"It was only going to be a marriage of convenience, *Dat,*" she said.

Now that she'd said it out loud, she realized how it must sound to her parents. She didn't like the sound of it, so she couldn't very well expect them to like it. Judging by the look of hurt in their eyes, she'd have to say it was the wrong thing to say.

"Let me explain," she said, hoping to undo the damage she'd just done by putting her foot in her mouth the way she had.

"There is nothing to discuss," her father said with a raised voice. "I will not tolerate disobedience from *mei dochder,*" her father said with a raised voice. "You made a commitment to the community to teach the *kinner,* and you will see that obligation through

175

until the end of the year; if you want to get married next wedding season, then you have my consent, but you do not have it now."

"But I'm already married, *Dat!* We just came from the Bishop's *haus, Dat,*" she said, her voice cracking.

"He married us just a few minutes ago," Luke spoke up.

Her father's face twisted with anger, and her mother left the room; that was never a good sign.

"I will go to the Bishop tomorrow, and I will have him annul the marriage," he said, his eyes narrowed.

Lettie backed up toward Luke. "I don't want my marriage annulled," she cried.

"Then, you will be shunned!" he hollered.

Lettie jumped at the roar of his voice.

"I will go to the Bishop and explain to him that you did *not* have my permission to marry and ask him to annul the marriage, and if you object, I will ask him to put you under

176

the ban, and you will lose the community *and* your *familye!"*

"*Nee,"* she cried. "Please don't do that; I love Luke, and I want to stay married to him."

"You can marry him in a year, or you won't be married to him at all," her father roared.

Lettie jumped again, but she felt Luke's hand at her elbow. "Maybe I should give you some time with your *familye,* and we can talk more tomorrow once everyone has had a chance to calm down," he said to her.

Everything in her wanted to plead with him not to leave her here, but he was her husband, and she would start their marriage off by showing him she trusted him to know what was best for them. The scriptures said in Proverbs that it was better for a man to live on the corner of his roof than to share his home with a quarrelsome wife; she did not intend to be a thorn in her husband's side. Even if she did leave with him now, she doubted they'd enjoy the evening they had planned, so perhaps it was best if she stayed here and tried to talk some sense into her father.

"I think it's wise of you to go home and leave Lettie here with her *familye*," her father said. "But I'm not going to change my mind about this; you and I can discuss the possibility of courting Lettie, but I won't consider letting you marry her for at least another year."

Anger filled Lettie, but not for Luke; she didn't have anything to say to her father for embarrassing her this way and treating her like a child instead of the married adult that she was.

CHAPTER THIRTEEN

Lettie rose earlier than she expected her parents to get up, hoping she could avoid any more talk about her doomed marriage to Luke. She was emotionally exhausted and didn't know if she could stomach any more confrontation from her father. After hours of lecturing her last night before he would allow her to retire for the evening, she'd gone to bed crying and missing Luke. Hours of battling for sleep gave her too much time to think, and she woke this morning determined to leave her parents and cling to her husband if that's what it took to save her marriage. She regretted not going with him last night and worried that he might have expected her to, even though he had given her an out. Had he used that *out* to let her go? She prayed not. If Luke could convince the Bishop to override her father's decision, then they could stay in the community, but she doubted her father would agree not to ban her if she did.

When she entered the kitchen, Annabelle was there making coffee. She looked up at Lettie's red-rimmed eyes and snickered. "I'm guessing you didn't have such a restful night," she said.

Her snotty tone made Lettie want to walk away from her and refuse to speak to her, but she would show her immature cousin a better example than that. If that didn't work, she'd shower her with kindness, heaping burning coals on her head the way it says in the Bible. She ignored her comment and refused to respond while she went over to the coffee pot and poured herself a cup.

"I'm also guessing your *vadder* shut down your plans to marry Luke," she said with a mean giggle.

A fire roared up from Lettie's stomach; what did Annabelle know about the events that unfolded last night?

Unless Annabelle knew that her parents were coming home.

"And I'm guessing you sent word to *mei vadder* about my plans to marry Luke," Lettie barked at her.

Annabelle put a hand to her chest and puffed out her bottom lip. "I was only trying to do what was best for you and save you from agreeing to a marriage of convenience."

"So, you were trying to spare me?"

She giggled. "Of course!"

Lettie glared at her. "I don't believe you!"

Annabelle sucked in her breath and then narrowed her eyes. "I won't have you calling me a liar!"

"I'm only stating a fact," Lettie said. "You have been trying to sabotage my plans with Luke all week. Honestly, Annabelle, I have no idea why you think you have to be the center of attention all the time and can't let anyone else have something you don't."

The young girl pursed her lips. "I can't have you getting married before me!"

"Maybe if you had a sweeter disposition and a bigger heart, then you might find yourself a match!"

"The matchmaker sent me over to Luke's *haus* last week, and *you* sabotaged what could have been my engagement supper with him! So, for that, I'm not about to let you take that away from me."

"Grow up, Annabelle, and stop thinking of yourself for once!" Lettie barked.

She turned on her heels and left the room; she would be late for school if she didn't get dressed and out the door, and she was not about to stick around the house long enough to suffer more insults and lectures from her father before she had to leave.

****

Lettie walked up to the school building just before the first student arrived. It had been a long walk, but she was not about to take her father's buggy or his horse today. Since she planned to go against his wishes for her future and go home with her husband, she determined it was best to leave it all behind her. She'd packed a small bag with a few of her things and set them outside the front door, planning on taking them with her when she left. It wasn't much, but it would be enough to get her started; she could make more dresses and personal linens for herself as time went on. She'd hoped to leave the house before her father came in from the barn to get his breakfast, but she hadn't managed to escape without getting some words of reprimand from him. She'd exited through the front door and taken her bag with her, and walked all the way to school without even saying goodbye to either her parents or Annabelle. She would have liked to have hugged her mother, but she was a grown and married woman, and it was time for her to get on with her future and put her childhood, including her family, behind her. Since her father had forced her to make a hard choice, she'd cried most of the way there, but sniffled back the tears as she approached the school. She had a class to teach, and she would leave her worries at the door.

Leaving her coat on, Lettie put her bag in the large bottom drawer of her desk, she went to the woodstove and lit the fire to warm the classroom. She was frozen to the bone, and her shoes were damp from the thick frost that covered the grass. Before long, she was warm enough to remove her coat but left her sweater on.

Lord, help me get through the day with the kinner and make it a gut day for them despite the sadness that fills my heart. Bless my marriage and don't let mei vadder or the Bishop put an end to it. You know my heart, Lord, and I love Luke and want to stay married to him. I want to be a mudder to Eli and Ellie. Danki, Amen.

The children put away their coats and began to assemble near their desks; peering into each of their faces; she couldn't believe how much she would miss each of them. But if she were able to keep her marriage with Luke, gaining two of those children as her own would more than make up for the loss. She had enjoyed teaching these past years, and she realized when faced with losing Luke that she would gladly give up teaching to be his wife.

Lettie turned her back on the class to put her last lesson plan for them on the chalkboard. She didn't want to think of today in terms of losing anything because she'd served well as a teacher to the students, and now it was time for her life to begin anew with a husband and children of her own.

The morning seemed to drag on, and Lettie had to scold herself several times for letting her thoughts drift to Luke. She went from nervous to anxious several times wondering if she'd see him today, or if he'd given up the way her father had ordered him to.

Just before the lunch hour, laughter erupted in her classroom, and she was almost afraid to turn around and address the source; she was certain Eli was behind it.

Within minutes, the children filled the classroom with chatter and laughter, and she hesitated to investigate the chaos until one of the female students let out a squeal. Turkey gobbling noises pricked her ears as she turned around to see what was going on.

In the back of the room, Eli was busy ushering a wild turkey toward the front of the room, and the sight of it made her bite her bottom lip to keep from laughing along with her class, thinking that his new teacher was going to have her hands full with him. Still, as his new mother, it would be her duty after today to keep him in line, and she would have to do her best to keep him from being a constant disruption. For now, she would deal with his actions as a teacher alone and not as his mother since he had no idea that she and Luke were married last night. They hadn't had the chance to talk to each other much about it, much less the children. If only her father hadn't ruined things with the help of her cousin.

"The turkey has to go outside!" Lettie said to Eli as she walked toward the back of her classroom, where he was wrangling the turkey toward the front of the room.

The frightened bird ran into a couple of the desks, spreading papers with his large wingspan as he tried to fly away from the boy and the other students. Lettie jumped into action, spreading her arms toward the animal, hoping it would back up, but it didn't.

"Open the door!" she squealed. "We have to get him out; everyone move to the other side of the room and slowly work your way to the front of the room. We need him to calm down because he's scared—more scared of us than we are of him."

The class did as they were told, except for Eli, who was still pushing the large bird toward her. Why was he working against her?

"Eli—back up so the turkey will go back outside," she ordered him.

"I want him to stay!" the boy whined.

"He has to go!" she said with an even louder voice.

Eli backed out of the way and skittered between the desks to get beside Lettie, and then helped her get the turkey to move toward the back of the classroom. It took some doing, but by the time they closed in on him, he'd ducked into the cloakroom.

"He's trapped!" Eli complained. "Now what are we going to do?"

Lettie took the boy's hand and led him back into the classroom area and stood her ground to keep the bird from coming back in. They stood in the gap between the cloakroom and the door leading to the schoolyard, but Lettie wasn't sure how they would coax him out of what he might deem as safety from the crazy schoolteacher and wayward child who were trying to turn him into Thanksgiving dinner. She'd been right when she'd warned the children that he was more afraid of them than they were of him, but she had no idea how to get the animal to understand she meant him no harm.

"How are we gonna get him out?" Eli asked, tugging on the sleeve of her sweater.

"I don't know; we might have to wait him out."

Before she could stop him, Eli darted into the entrance of the cloakroom, and the turkey began to squawk and flap his massive wings, knocking coats from the pegs and causing lunch pails to drop from the shelf onto the floor where the contents spilled out.

"He's wrecking out lunches!" Eli squealed.

"Get out of there, Eli, and leave him alone," Lettie said, reaching around the corner and grabbing his hand.

"I'm trying to get him out, I promise," he cried.

"Let's leave him alone," Lettie said. "In the meantime, help me line up the desks in the doorway so he can't get back into the classroom."

Eli did as he was told, and a couple of the older students came over to help. Once they had themselves barricaded in, she ordered the children to let themselves out the back door beside her desk, hoping that it would make the turkey calm down enough to leave the building.

****

Luke walked away from Annabelle and went about his chores in the barn, the young girl close on his heels.

"Leave me alone, Annabelle, I have chores to do, and then I have to go have lunch with *mei fraa* because school is about to let out for the noon hour."

"*Ach,* if I know *mei onkel,* he's at the Bishop's *haus* right now getting your marriage annulled," she said with a mean giggle.

"It isn't your *onkel's* decision to have our marriage annulled," Luke barked. "Lettie won't let that happen any more than I will."

He intended to go to the Bishop and plead with him after he talked to Lettie over lunch. He was anxious to see her and prayed she would agree with him to keep the marriage whatever the cost—even if meant excommunication from the community.

Annabelle smirked. "Lettie won't have any choice in the matter. *Mei onkel* is a pretty strict *mann,* and once he gets something in his head, he's determined to see it through."

"Did her *vadder* send you over here to try to convince me to have my marriage annulled?"

She shrugged and flashed him an innocent look. "He might have suggested I come over here to talk to you, but I was willing!" She smiled and sauntered a little closer, but Luke backed away. "If you want to, we can go over to the Bishop's *haus,* and I'm willing to marry you so you'll have a *fraa* and a *mudder* for the *kinner.*"

"Nee, I'm already married," he said with a raised voice. "Lettie is the only woman I'll ever love, and she is the best choice for a *mudder* for the *kinner.* You're too young, and I don't care for you."

"I thought all you wanted was a marriage of convenience!" she squealed.

"I'm not discussing my personal life with you, Annabelle, so you can go back to your *onkel* and tell him his little trick to distract me away from Lettie didn't work."

"You know *mei* cousin doesn't want to give up teaching," Annabelle said. "I heard her telling *mei onkel* this morning when I went over there for breakfast."

Luke's heart faltered behind his ribs; surely, this girl was trying to get under his skin, and he couldn't let her. Still, Lettie had been crying when he'd shown up last night

"You *knew* her parents were coming home?" he asked.

She laughed. "Of course I knew; I'm the one who called over to Annie's barn and told them they needed to come home and stop Lettie's foolish behavior. I knew the rule her *vadder* set down for her, but she seemed to have forgotten that she is to honor her *vadder* and *mudder.* So all I did was to save her from making a big mistake and getting herself shunned by her *vadder. Ach,* I did her a favor!"

"I think you tried to do yourself a favor, but I'll wait another year to have her for *mei fraa,* I'd rather wait for Lettie before I'd agree to marry you!" he grumbled. "So, if you'll excuse me, I have chores to do so that I can go pick up *mei fraa* and *kinner* from the school and bring them home where they belong."

Annabelle sucked in a breath and huffed as she turned on her heels. "You'll be begging me to marry you before the day is over!" she said over her shoulder as she walked back to her buggy.

"Don't count on it!" he hollered after her.

Luke leaned against the horse stall in the barn to steady his shaky legs while he listened for buggy wheels to indicate that Annabelle was leaving. He drew in a deep breath and blew it out. What if the girl was right and her father had already been to the Bishop's house to have their marriage annulled? Could he do that?

Luke felt sick to his stomach; why had he left last night without his bride? He thought it was best not to go against her father and to give her time to talk to him, but thinking back on it now, he wished he would have insisted she go with him.

****

Lettie folded her arms and stared at Eli. "What were you thinking, letting that turkey in the classroom? Someone could have gotten seriously hurt."

"I'm sorry," he said. "Does this mean you're going to have to talk to *Onkel* Luke?"

"Not if you promise to behave," Lettie assured him.

"But you *have* to talk to him," Eli whined. "You can't punish me because you're not *mei mamm*—yet."

She was tempted to tell him she was, but it wasn't the right time.

"I don't want to punish you," she said.

Eli lowered his head and began to cry. "Does this mean you won't talk to *Onkel* Luke?"

"Why is it so important for you that I talk to your *Onkel* Luke?"

"I overheard *Onkel* Luke saying he went to the matchmaker instead of asking you to marry him like he promised our *dat,*" Eli answered. "So I thought if I was bad in school, you'd have to talk to him, and it would remind him he's supposed to marry you."

Lettie stared at the boy. Cassie was right; they did have their own agenda because she'd just gotten outwitted by a second grader! But what about his worries? Luke had told her last night before leaving her doorstep not to say anything to the children today because he thought it was best if they told them together, and she'd agreed, but after her encounter with her father, they'd forgotten about telling them. Now she worried that keeping it from the poor child would be just short of torture.

"Is that why you've been misbehaving the past few days?"

He nodded. "I wanted you to be my *mamm.*"

Lettie considered telling Eli to let him off the hook, but perhaps playing along with him would be best. "Alright, I guess I'll have to take you home after school and have a talk with your *Onkel* Luke about your conduct in the classroom today."

The turkey waddled out of the building, and Lettie ordered the children back inside.

She tapped Eli on the shoulder. "Now that the turkey is gone, I'd appreciate it if you'd clean up the mess he made."

His eyes lit up when she promised to take him home, and he was all too eager to clean up after the chaos the turkey had created, but she had a hunch he thought it had been worth it.

****

Luke pulled his buggy up in front of the school prepared to claim his bride but filled with fear that he would not be able to. He grabbed the wildflowers he'd gathered along the way and walked inside the school where only Lettie and the twins remained; all the other children were gone.

"What happened here?" he asked as he walked over a big pile of rubble. He handed Lettie the flowers and winked at her, bringing a smile to her pink lips.

"It's all my fault," Eli admitted.

"You were awfully fast to speak up," Luke said, rubbing the top of the boy's head with his palm. "Are you proud of yourself for this mess?"

He shook his head.

"How did it happen?"

Luke was happy that Lettie walked away to give him some privacy with Eli even though he was eager to see her and even more anxious to talk to her.

"Did you see the turkey running around in the schoolyard?" Eli asked.

Luke nodded. "Don't tell me you let the turkey come in here!"

Luke glanced over at Lettie, who was nodding and covering a smile with her hand. He pursed his lips to keep from smiling back and confusing the boy into thinking he might approve of his antics.

"Do you mind telling me why?" Luke demanded, turning his attention to Eli.

"Because I didn't want the matchmaker to find you someone else to be our *mudder,"* he said with a whiny voice.

Luke crouched down on his haunches and put his arm around the twins. "You don't have to pull a stunt like this ever again because I'm here to bring Miss Fisher—your new *mudder* home with us," he said, standing upright and beckoning her over to them. "That is if she'll still have me."

"Say yes!" the twins begged.

Lettie smiled eagerly and joined him and the twins in a group hug.

After a few minutes, Luke put a firm hand on Eli's shoulder. "Let's get this mess cleaned up so we can go home."

"What are we going to do about the turkey?" the boy asked. "Can we take him home with us?"

Luke nodded. "If he's still out there when we finish cleaning up this mess."

"What can I name this one?" Eli asked with an innocent smile.

"I'm going name this one," Luke interrupted him. "His name is Thanksgiving dinner!"

Eli laughed. "Okay, but you have to save Bishop and *Frau* Gobbler so they can make more turkeys for next year."

Luke smirked. "We'll come back tomorrow to catch that turkey; I have a feeling he's here looking for his friends. I hadn't planned on raising turkeys, but it's not a bad idea; you've got yourself a couple of pets with Bishop and *Frau* Gobbler, but if they don't have any little turkeys by next year, they're going on the table for supper!"

Eli frowned. "I'll have to ask the Bishop if he can marry them when he marries you and Miss Fisher so we can have little turkeys next year for Thanksgiving."

Lettie bit her bottom lip to smile at the boy who was about to be her child, and she could already see that she was going to have to persuade Luke to have a talk with him about the *Birds and the Bees*.

CHAPTER FOURTEEN

Lettie stopped writing the lesson plan on the board for the new teacher long enough to watch Luke with the children. They'd made fast work of cleaning the mess, and they were nearly finished. Eli was almost like a reverse tornado trying to get the messes straightened so he could take his new mother home. She had a hunch he was hoping for some home-baked cookies to eat before he went to bed tonight, but she was going to have to disappoint him their first night as a family. If she knew her mother, the woman would have spent an emotional day baking cookies, pies, and cakes. She'd prayed for her mother to let go of her addiction to sugary treats, but she baked when she was upset, and Lettie's argument with her father over her marriage to Luke had upset her greatly.

Lettie would have to double-check with Luke first, but she prayed he'd go along with her plan to stop by her parent's farm on the way home. She didn't want things to end this way with them; she wanted them to be a part of their lives and especially the children's lives. They needed grandparents just as much as she needed to keep her parents in her life. She couldn't see going through motherhood without the guidance of her mother, and she didn't want to.

Lettie finished the last assignment and put down the stick of chalk and clapped her hands together to clear the chalk dust from them. Luke had snuffed out the fire in the woodstove, and she motioned him toward her so they could have a moment with the children within earshot.

He reached for her hands, and she gave them to him freely; the warmth of them sent tingles coursing through her. She'd be a fool to let him go again when she loved him so much it hurt to think of spending even another minute away from him. Her arms had ached for him last night when she was tossing about trying to rid herself of anxiety so she could sleep.

"I've missed you," he offered.

She giggled. "I missed you too."

"I got a visit from your cousin just before I came here," Luke began. "She told me she was the one who alerted your parents about our engagement; why would she do that?"

Lettie resisted the urge to roll her eyes at the mention of her cousin. "She told me too; I think she's proud of herself, and I don't understand why she would do such a thing except that Cassie thinks she's jealous of me. She had the nerve to tell me this morning that she couldn't have me getting married before her—like getting married was a competition or something. She always was a *mean girl.*"

"Ach, she practically begged me to have our marriage annulled so I could marry her instead."

Lettie blew out a breath. "She's ambitious, isn't she?"

"That, and a few other things!" he answered. "She did warn me that your *vadder* probably talked to the Bishop to get him to annul our marriage; I know he threatened it last night before I left, but would he really go through with that?"

"I wouldn't speak to him this morning before I left for school, so I don't know," she said, tears clogging her throat.

"I think we should pay the Bishop a visit after we leave here," he said. "I thought about going there before I came here, but I thought it might be better for us to go together."

"Danki, I'm glad you want me to go with you. I'm sorry I let you leave last night; I should have gone with you."

"Does that mean that if your *vadder* still objects to our marriage, you'll stay *mei fraa?"*

She nodded and forced a smile. "*Jah,* I will because I love you; I only wish *mei vadder* wasn't forcing me to choose between you. But you are my husband, and I choose you."

Luke smile and squeezed her hands; she could see in his eager eyes that he wanted to hold her and kiss her, but now was not the time for that with the children in such close proximity, though she felt the same way.

"After we leave the Bishop's *haus,*" she said. "Can we go to visit my parents? I want to give *mei dat* one more chance to welcome you to his *familye.* If he turns us away, then I'll be able to walk away knowing that I gave him every chance to keep from shunning me."

Luke nodded. "I agree; we'll go and give him a chance, but I'm happy to hear that you will stand by me in this marriage."

"*Danki.* I have no intention of going back on the vows I made to you last night; I love you," she said, lowering her voice so the children wouldn't overhear her.

"I love you too, Lettie," he whispered.

They stared into each other's eyes for several minutes and smiled before Eli broke the spell between them.

"We're done!" "Eli announced with pride in his voice. "Can we go home now?"

Lettie examined the classroom, noting how clean it was—almost better than it was when she'd arrived this morning. "I hope you learned your lesson," she said.

"I promise I won't be bad anymore to get *Onkel* Luke to marry you," the boy said.

Luke ruffled his hair. "You won't have to because I married Lettie—Miss Fisher, last night, so she's Lettie King now, but *Mamm* to the two of you!"

"*Mamm!*" The twins rushed to her and hugged her, shouts of joy bringing tears to her eyes.

It suddenly hit her that she was a mother and a wife, and she was going to make a good life with Luke and the twins. They walked out of the school, and she didn't even look back; teaching was in her past. Being a wife and mother was the only future she wanted.

****

Luke drove his buggy with his family to the Bishop's house, hoping they could get some answers. He didn't want to get shunned for his marriage to Lettie, and he prayed the Bishop would not override his own decision to marry them last night after a visit from Lettie's angry and unyielding father. He reached for her hand, and she surrendered it to him with a sad smile. He wished they didn't have to start their marriage off this way, but if they didn't take care of it once and for all, they would not be able to move past it.

"I'm sorry for all the trouble this has caused you," he said, leaning in and whispering in her ear how much he loved her.

"We're in this together," she said.

"For better or for worse," he added. "But let's start praying for *Gott's* blessings over our marriage and our *familye* so that we can live in peace."

"Amen to that!" Lettie said with a light giggle.

When they arrived at the Bishop's house, the twins jumped out of the buggy and raced each other down to the lake, and Lettie was grateful they would be out of earshot of the adult conversation.

The Bishop welcome Luke and Lettie to join him on the back porch since it was such a pleasant day, but his strange smile worried Lettie. After they were seated, his wife offered them some refreshments. He nodded to her and then turned his attention to his guests.

"Don't tell me you're here to get your marriage annulled," he said, directing his gaze toward Lettie. "Because I already told your *vadder,* I'm not in the business to undo what *Gott* has joined together."

She and Luke shook their heads, but Lettie swallowed down a lump in her throat. "*Mei vadder* paid you a visit and asked you to undo our marriage?"

Tears welled up in her eyes when he nodded, a discouraging look in his eyes.

"When I refused, he asked me to issue the ban over the two of you. He became angry with me when I refused that request too. Did the two of you do something you need to confess, or is he acting like an over-protective *vadder?*"

"*Nee,*" Lettie said. "He had forbidden me to marry before I was twenty-five; after what Annie did by leaving the community to marry, he didn't want me to do the same. He also told me I'd made a commitment to the school and couldn't marry until next wedding season because of that."

The Bishop nodded. "*Jah,* that's the excuse he gave me, too, but I told him I already found a replacement teacher, and she's supposed to start tomorrow."

Lettie nodded, realizing for the first time, the mention of her not teaching had not filled her with dread. She glanced at Luke, who was now her whole life, and she was happy, though she'd be happier once the strife between her and her father could end.

"Is there anything you would advise us to do besides try to talk to him?" Luke asked.

"I recommend talking to him as soon as possible," The Bishop said.

"We planned on going there as soon as we left your place," Luke informed him.

"That's probably best; I suggested to him that he pray about the situation and open his heart to the *familye* he's gaining," the Bishop said.

His wife came out to the porch with meadow tea and cookie. "Is it alright if I take some cookies and milk to the *kinner,*" *Frau* Troyer asked, aiming her question at Lettie. "I don't want to spoil their supper."

Lettie shook her head. "We had a late lunch because of a mishap at the school, which caused me to have to dismiss early, and I have a feeling it's going to be late before we get any supper tonight."

"What happened at the school?" the Bishop asked with a raised eyebrow. "Anything that I will have to do damage-control with the parents?"

Lettie shook her head. "*Nee,* a wild turkey got inside the school and messed it up, but we stayed there and put everything back in order before we left, and I took the time to write the lesson plan for the week on the chalkboard for the new teacher, so when she walks in the class tomorrow, she won't notice anything different."

The Bishop took a sip of his tea and set his cup down. "I'm glad to hear that, but how did the turkey get into the building?"

"That's a long story," Lettie began, but Luke interrupted to let her off the hook.

"Eli thought he needed to let the turkey in to get Lettie's attention, hoping if he got into trouble, she'd have to talk to me and it would remind me that I'm supposed to marry her," he said. "But we told them about our marriage after deciding between us that if we were to get shunned, we would stay in the marriage and keep the commitment we made to each other."

Lettie nodded, and the Bishop gave a nod.

"I'm happy to hear that you're both committed to the marriage," he said. "It makes my job easier; I was only prepared to annul the marriage if the two of you decided that was what you wanted, and I knew I had to speak with the two of you first. I didn't want to so firm with your *vadder,* Lettie, but he had to know it was the decision of the two of you and then for me to agree. But like I told him, I don't believe in undoing what *Gott* has joined any more than I believe in divorce. I had a feeling that neither of you wanted an annulment since you came to me so eagerly wanting to be married. I want you to enjoy your life together; I will pray that your *vadder* will come around to the idea of your marriage and *familye.* When I reminded him that he had *grandkinner* to think about now, it sparked a little bit of hope in his eyes. He and your *mudder* enjoyed themselves during their extended visit with your *schweschder* and their *grandkinner* there."

"The twins brought us together," Luke said with a chuckle. "So I have a feeling their witty behavior will help them to earn favor with their new pappy."

"Those two are quite the little charmers despite everything they've been through," the

Bishop agreed. "But having a new *familye* will be the best thing to heal those wounds of theirs. I have a feeling they'll bounce back very quickly once the two of you settle into a routine with them. I have a feeling Eli won't be getting into as much trouble at school after today, either."

Lettie looked out toward the lake and smiled at the twins' whimsical playing. "I have a feeling his troublesome days are over."

The twins came bounding onto the back porch and set their empty cups and napkins on the table and ran back down to the lake; it did Lettie's heart good to see them so happy despite the recent tragedy in their lives.

"They're very well-adjusted," the Bishop agreed. "I know your *brudder* did everything he could to prepare them for what was to come after his diagnosis, and I think it might have made things easier on them to have you with them, Luke."

Luke nodded and forced a smile, trying not to show that he was still hurting from the loss of his brother.

"Let them do the talking for you when you visit your folks, Lettie," the Bishop suggested. "I have a feeling they'll get farther than you will; your *vadder* won't argue in front of the *kinner,* and he won't start one in front of them. Use that to your advantage, but be willing to speak up about your side of things. I can see how much the two of you love each other; let him see that too, and things will work out for you. It might take some time for him to fully come around to the idea of having both of his *dochders* married, but it will come with time and patience from you."

"*Danki,* Bishop," Lettie said, sipping the rest of her tea. It was a nice pick-me-up after the crazy day she'd had.

****

After bidding the Bishop and his wife a pleasant afternoon and thanking them for the hospitality, Luke settled into the front seat of his buggy next to his wife and set his horse in motion toward her parents' farm.

"Are you ready to take on the world right now?" he asked her with a chuckle. "I have a feeling the Bishop had something there about using the *kinner* as a smokescreen."

Lettie giggled; she didn't want to admit it, but it was a good idea. She wasn't one to stand behind a couple of children and let them do her bidding, but she had a feeling they could work their charms on her father the same way they had won her over and broken down the barriers between her and Luke. Those two were very persuasive, and if they weren't careful, they might have their hands full when the twins were old enough to go on *rumspringa*.

The late afternoon sun sank below the tree line, and Lettie shivered just a little. She reached in the back of the buggy for her sweater, but Luke put his arm around her, which to her, was much better than the lifeless garment. She would have no trouble getting used to having someone care for her needs and acting on them before she voiced them.

"Do you think your *mamm* might offer to feed us?" Luke asked. "I missed lunch because of someone's antics at the school, and the snack at the Bishop's *haus* wasn't enough to wet my whistle."

Lettie shrugged. "I suppose that will depend on *mei vadder's* mood. If things don't go well, I'm sure we won't be there long, and we can eat something when we get back to your farm."

"Back to *our* farm," he corrected her.

She giggled. "That might take some getting used to, but I like the sound of it."

"Let's turn the twins loose on him when we get there, so your *mudder* will extend an invitation to supper," he whispered in her ear. "I'd hate to have you cooking on our wedding night. If we eat there, we can go straight home and put the twins to bed and have the rest of the evening to ourselves; I can build us a fire."

His warm breath in her ear made her shiver and let out a giggle; she liked the idea of sitting in front of a warm fire with her husband and not having to worry about stopping herself when she wanted more than kisses from her. She smiled inwardly, but she could feel the heat creeping up her neck, her heart pounding out of control.

Lord, bless us to get through the evening with mei parents. Soften mei vadder's heart so he will accept my marriage and the twins as his grandkinner. If it is your will, let me spend some time in the kitchen with mei mudder once more so she can give me some advice about my impending wedding night with Luke. Give mei vadder a heart for Luke and help them to form a familye bond. I pray that he will be calm when we arrive so we can mend fences. Open his eyes to the love that Luke and I have for one another, and let there be no more talk from his lips about annulling our marriage or shunning us. Danki, Amen.

Lettie settled in beside her husband and leaned her head on his shoulder as she enjoyed the sound of the birds along the country road in which they traveled. He was in no hurry to get where they were going, and she was content with that. The gelding moved at a leisurely pace, and the rhythmic clip-clop of his hooves and the grinding of the buggy wheels relaxed her almost to a state of sleepiness. She hadn't slept much last night, and she suspected she might not get much sleep tonight either, but she was more than content with that.

CHAPTER FIFTEEN

Lettie got the shakes when Luke pulled his buggy into the driveway at her parents' house, but she stiffened her frame, hoping to hide it from her husband. He had enough to worry about without having to coddle her during a visit to her parents that likely gave him the shakes too. She'd been so comfortable in his arms all the way there that she'd actually dozed off, and though it had given her a much-needed second wind, she was suddenly filled with a bit of anxiousness.

"Everything is going to work out according to *Gott's* plan," Luke assured her.

"So, don't fret. I'm planning to have a pleasant meal and visit with your *familye,* but if it doesn't work out that way, it'll be fine either way."

She nodded. "You're right; I said a lengthy prayer on the way here, so I have to trust that *Gott* knows what is best for us."

He winked at her and smiled; she wished he could kiss her, but now was not the time. If her father witnessed a display of affection between them, it might set things off in the wrong direction, and he would ruin the evening with his mood. Better to keep things on an old-fashioned level tonight for the sake of making peace.

"Can we stay outside and play until it gets too dark?" Eli begged.

"There's some new kittens in the barn," Lettie said. "I know they are ready to leave their *mamm* now, so if it's alright with your *Onkel* Luke, you can go out there and pick one to take home."

Luke chuckled. "Might want to pick out two; we could always use a couple of new barn cats."

The twins' wide eyes and smiles brought joy to Lettie's heart, and they wasted no time running out toward the barn. It was probably best if they stayed out of earshot of any potentially raised words from her father. She prayed that by the time he calmed down and could be reasoned with, it would be safe for the children to join them. They'd been through enough trauma, and she didn't want them to suffer through another stern lecture from her father, and she didn't want them to know he objected to her being their mother. To hear such a thing could make them feel unwanted, and that was no way to begin her life as their mother.

Luke squeezed her hand. "Are you ready, *Frau* King?"

She smiled, thinking that hearing her new name was like listening to a song coming from his lips to her ears. "*Jah,* I'm as ready as I'll ever be."

They stood on the front porch, and Lettie blew out a breath with a whoosh before she knocked. Her father opened the door and pursed his lips, but invited them in. She bit her bottom lip when they entered through the front room as she remembered many nights curled up on the sofa with Annie while they listened to their father reading from the Bible, a warm fire, and the lull of his voice lulling them to sleep. From the kitchen, the aroma of *Snitz* pie tickled her nose, the strong scent of cinnamon, giving away her mother's passion for baking as a means of calming her became evident. She hated to think that her mother had been held up in the kitchen for the last twenty-four hours, baking everything she could to get rid of her anxiety; the sooner they settled things between them, the better off her mother's emotional health would be.

"Why don't you go join your *mudder* in the kitchen and see if you can get her to put away her baking pans and make some supper while I take your young *mann* outside on the porch and have a talk with him," her father said.

Lettie flashed Luke a worrisome look, but he smiled, letting her know he was going to be okay alone with her father. She gave him a quick nod and left them to their talk while she strolled into the kitchen to see if she could persuade her mother to stop baking long enough to talk with her. She needed some motherly advice, and the woman would be in no shape to give it to her if she was a complete mess.

She closed the space between them and kissed her mother lightly on the cheek she offered her, hugging her with one arm to keep flour from getting all over the place. Judging by the array of baked goods lining the counters, she'd spent most of the day in the kitchen.

"Are you going to let me take any of this *home* with me?" she said, careful not to put too much emphasis on the word *home.* Her mother was more understanding than her father, but she also knew she stood by her husband.

"Jah, take what you want,*"* her mother said with a smile. "Does your *vadder* know you're here?"

Lettie nodded. "He let us in."

"*Us?*"

"*Jah,* he took Luke outside on the porch so they could talk," Lettie said. "He isn't going to make me a widow, is he?"

Her mother chuckled. "*Nee,* he's calmed down quite a bit after his meeting with the Bishop. That *mann* is set in his ways and doesn't want to hear that he's wrong; I was happy to let him go and talk to the Bishop alone this morning so he could let it all out. I figured if I went along, even if I stayed in the kitchen with Miriam, he might not be able to talk freely, so I stayed home and baked—and prayed."

Lettie nodded and smiled at her mother; she was a wise woman, and she admired her a great deal. It took a strong-willed woman to put up with her father's moods all these years, and her mother always kept a calm spirit of cheerfulness about her no matter how irritable he became. Baking was her outlet, but Lettie knew she used that time to talk with God and work things out in her mind and heart.

"We went to talk to the Bishop before we came here," Lettie said, grabbing a plastic baggie from the drawer nearest the stove and began tucking away some cookies in it for the twins. "I was disappointed to hear that he went over there to talk the Bishop into shunning us and annulling the marriage."

"I'm sorry he did that," she said, excusing her husband's behavior.

She was always making excuses for him and apologizing for him; just once, Lettie would appreciate it if the man would say it for himself. He was old and set in his ways, but that didn't mean a man couldn't change, did it?

"I begged him to think about it before he did that, but you know how stubborn he is," her mother went on.

Lettie put away most of the baked goods in the pantry and then checked the refrigerator to see if her mother had anything prepared yet for supper. She noted the prepped chicken on a plate that her father had likely butchered and dressed not too long ago, but had tucked it away in the refrigerator since her mother was too preoccupied with baking.

"Do you want me to put this chicken in the oven for you, *Mamm?*" she asked. "I can peel some potatoes too; you've got plenty of biscuits made, and it'll make a nice meal."

Her mother hesitated as she looked around at the mess she'd made of her kitchen. Though Lettie had put away most of it, the counters were still littered with utensils and items in need of washing and putting away.

She started to sigh but turned it into a smile. "*Jah,* I'm sure your *vadder* would rather have chicken for supper than pie and cookies!"

She giggled at the thought of her father trading in his meat-and-potatoes appetite for three courses of sweets for supper, and she just didn't see that going over very well. From what she could see, this was the most baking her mother had done in one day since her sister, Annie, ran off and married in another community. Her father had been angry with Annie too, but as soon as the first grandchild was born, he welcomed his son-in-law. Luke came with two instant grandchildren; would that make Luke's wait for acceptance shorter than Annie's husband? She prayed it would.

****

Luke stared out at the cornfield, the dry stalks crackling in the breeze; he considered offering to help his father-in-law till them under before the first snow, but he thought it better to keep quiet until the man opened the conversation. He had an agenda, and Luke was eager to get the discussion underway.

"You and Lettie have a troubled past," Mr. Fisher began.

"*Jah,* we had a long talk about that, but I apologized, and she forgave me for causing her to break her arm," Luke interjected.

"I'm glad she finally forgave you; she's been holding onto that grudge for too many years." Mr. Fisher said. "But you know I'm against Lettie being married at this age,"

Luke nodded. "She told me that."

"I had a set of rules for *mei dochders,* and they've both broken them now. I wanted them to be old enough to know what they were getting into and who they were marrying, and I didn't want Lettie marrying out of convenience or obligation. Her happiness is my only concern; I feel that you undermined my authority and tricked my *dochder* into marrying you out of convenience."

He paused, but Luke didn't dare say a word; he would keep quiet until the man finished getting off his chest what he had to say.

Mr. Fisher blew out a breath and cupped his hands together in front of him, leaning his elbows on his knees and staring out at the cornfield. "I sympathize with your situation, Luke, and having to raise your *brudder's kinner* alone, but you and that *kinner* are not Lettie's responsibility. I feel that you should court her until next wedding season to give yourselves time to get to know one another and see if you love each other. That would give Lettie a chance to know her own heart."

Another pause and Luke waited for a signal that the man wanted a response out of him. He nodded as if giving him permission to speak. Luke swallowed, tucking his hands under his thighs to keep from raking his fingers through his hair. He had to stay calm, and fidgeting was not the way to show maturity or confidence.

"I've always wanted Lettie for my *fraa,*" Luke said. "I've loved her since we were in school together. I was unsure of Lettie's feelings until she shared them with me a couple of days ago. I didn't want to marry her out of convenience either; I even went to the matchmaker to find me another match because I didn't want to hurt her that way, and I didn't think she'd have me. But Lettie told me she felt the same way about me. When she told me she loved me, I knew this was not a marriage of convenience. If you want to know how she really feels, or that I'm telling the truth, I would ask that you speak to Lettie privately and ask her how she feels about me when I'm not around; that way, you can get her full and honest opinion of me without me influencing her in any way."

"I planned on talking to her without you," he said. "That way, I won't have to worry if she will hold back the truth from me if you're sitting right there."

Luke nodded; he completely agreed with the man.

"I think I'll go inside and check on the women and see if they have any supper cooking yet," Mr. Fisher said. "You might want to check on the *kinner* to make sure they're not getting into any trouble in the barn."

"I will," he said, rising from the chair. "*Danki,* I hope our talk has set your mind more at ease about my marriage to Lettie."

"It pleases me to know that you love *mei dochder,* but I need to make sure she feels the same way about you before I give my blessing over your marriage."

Luke nodded. "I understand, and I appreciate you giving me a chance."

Without another word, the man went inside the house, leaving Luke on the porch; he felt confident that he was about to get a blessing from Lettie's father. For now, he would go out to the barn and check on the twins.

****

Lettie finished peeling the last potato and cut it, dropping the quartered chunks into the pot of water with the rest of them. Her father entered the room just then and asked her to sit down with him at the table. Her heart skipped a beat, and she wondered where Luke was, but as she passed by the kitchen window, she spotted him walking into the barn. She prayed he wasn't fetching the twins so they could get in the buggy and leave her here with her parents. She blew out a breath, trusting that her prayers were about to be answered and God had softened her father's heart toward her husband, and instead of going back to the Bishop's house for an annulment, they'd all be sitting down to supper like a family within the hour.

She dried her hands on a kitchen towel and cracked the oven door to check on the chicken before taking a seat in the chair across from her father.

He looked at her with concern in his soft brown eyes and tugged on his long, white beard.

"I'm not going to pretend that I'm not worried about your sudden marriage to Luke," he said, breaking the silence between them. "I need to know how you really feel about him; did you marry Luke because you felt sorry for the twins, or did you feel obligated in any way to marry him?"

"*Nee, Dat,* I love him, I've always loved him," Lettie said. "I was upset when I thought he wanted a marriage of convenience, and even went to the matchmaker for it instead of coming and courting me. I always thought we were meant to be married, and I hoped someday that he would propose to me. When he went to the matchmaker, it broke my heart, but he did it because he didn't know I've loved him all this time. But in fairness to him, I didn't know how he felt about me either. I knew I loved him, but it would have broken my heart if he never returned that love. It turns out that we've secretly loved each other since we were in school together. He makes me happy. I have taught Eli and Ellie for the past two years, and I've grown to love them—not just as my students, but as a mother would love them. I've prayed to *Gott* if it was *gut* in his eyes and if this was where he wanted me to be—with Luke and the *kinner,* to open this door for me, and if not, that he would close it. I prayed just the way you taught me to pray, and *Gott* opened the door for my marriage to Luke. I'm the happiest I've been in my whole life, *Dat,* and the only one who stands in the way of that happiness is you."

"You talk like a mature woman instead of my little girl," her father said with a sense of sadness to his tone. "I suppose it's time I accepted that you're grown up and capable of making your own choices. I'm proud of you for following your heart, and I'm glad that you're happy because, as a *vadder,* your happiness is important to me. But I don't like the fact that Luke married you behind my back."

"That was my doing," Lettie admitted. "I knew you would object and so I pushed for a short engagement and an immediate wedding. Even the Bishop wanted to perform the ceremony when he did. It was Luke who wanted to wait; he asked me if I wanted to wait until you and *mamm* came home, and I told him no. I'm sorry, *Dat,* for disobeying you, but I love Luke, and I want to stay married to him. I want to raise the twins as my own *kinner,* and I pray that *Gott* will bless us with a *boppli* of our own."

She hadn't thought about having children with Luke, but it was suddenly a heartfelt need for her to complete her family with a child of her own. Her sister had told her after the birth of her first child that giving birth was something that every woman should experience.

Her father cleared his throat. "Then I have no choice but to give you my blessing—but it's with reservations."

Lettie's breath hitched. She didn't care that his blessing probably came with a long list of conditions; she bound from her chair and threw her arms around him with a half-giggle, half-cry.

"*Danki, Dat,*" she said.

Her mother came over to them and joined them in a hug; her father hadn't let go of the stern look that soured his face, but Lettie wasn't about to let it bother her. She had a hunch he didn't entirely believe that she could love Luke—especially given the fact that up until the time they'd left for Grabill to visit her sister, she'd bad-mouthed Luke constantly. Time would prove to her father that God had broken through the wall she'd put up between herself and Luke, but love had broken it down, and she didn't intend to let it back up. Forgiveness had softened her heart and replaced it with the love she'd always had for her husband, and nothing could change that.

Her father rose from the table and looked around at the sea of backed goods still littering the kitchen. "Maybe now your *mudder* will stop baking. After supper, you can take most of it home with you so I won't eat it. The *kinner* can run off those sweet treats easier than I can at my age."

Lettie smiled at the mention of her taking the cookies and pies *home* with her; it was a start in the right direction, wasn't it? At least he was acknowledging she had a home with Luke, and he was no longer insisting she stay in his house and leave her husband.

Though an apology would be nice for trying to have her marriage annulled, or even an admission that he was wrong, but she was content to settle for the lack of animosity between them for the time being. Perhaps in time, he'd admit he should have trusted her to make the right decision for her future.

"Why don't you women take a break and sit on the porch for a bit and get out of this hot kitchen," her father suggested. "I think we should sit outside and have a nice visit before supper."

Lettie agreed because she was eager to tell Luke the good news that her father had given them his blessing to stay married. On the porch, Luke and the twins were sitting on the swing, waiting for her.

Her father exited the house in front of her and extended a hand to Luke. He stood and shook her father's hand, which put a smile on Lettie's face.

"I'd like to give you my blessing for your marriage to *mei dochder,*" he said to Luke.

"*Danki,* that means a lot to me," Luke said.

"Does this mean you're going to be our pappy?" Eli asked her father.

The man nodded and smiled. "Indeed it does, but you also get a *Mammi,*" he said, pointing to Lettie's mother.

Tears filled Lettie's eyes as she watched the excitement in the twins' faces, and if she looked really hard, she could almost detect a twinkle in her father's eyes.

The twins bounced on their heels and begged her father to go and see the kittens they'd picked out until they wore him down; much to Lettie's surprise, he agreed to indulge them. They each took one of his hands and led him toward the barn; Lettie's breath hitched when the twins turned around and flashed her their mischievous smiles. They'd managed to find that iceberg in her father's heart and melted it when she'd spent her lifetime chipping away at it and hadn't made as much progress as they had in only a few minutes.

Once again, Lettie had been outwitted by a couple of children, but this time, she didn't mind it at all.

THE END

PLEASE FOLLOW ME

BookBub

FACEBOOK

TWITTER

MY BLOG

PINTEREST

INSTAGRAM

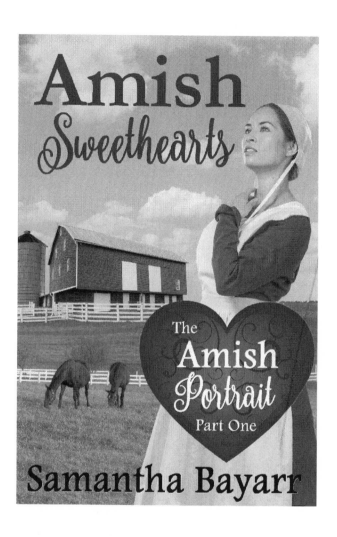

Amish Sweethearts

The Amish Portrait Part One

Samantha Bayarr

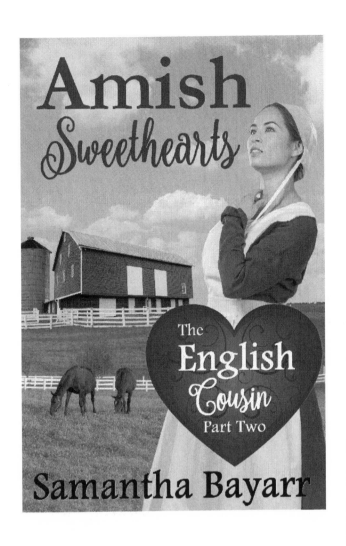

Amish *Sweethearts*

The **English** *Cousin* Part Two

Samantha Bayarr

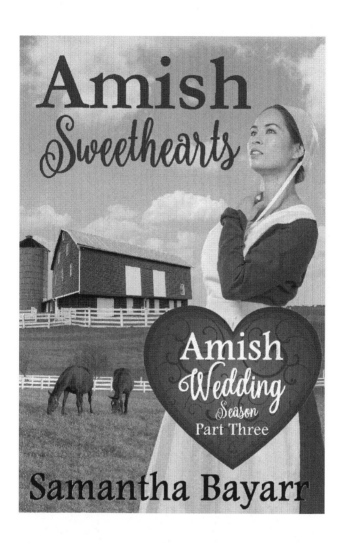

Amish
Sweethearts

Amish
Wedding
Season
Part Three

Samantha Bayarr

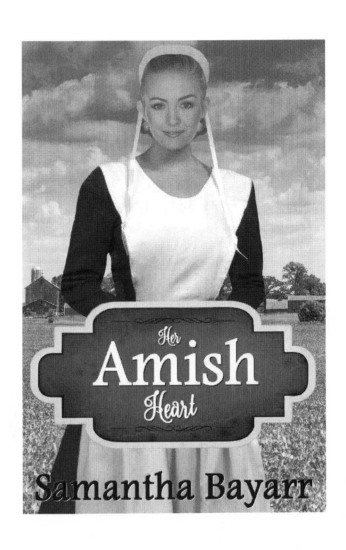

Amish
Christmas Bakery

Samantha Bayarr

Made in the USA
Middletown, DE
13 November 2019

78631289R00144